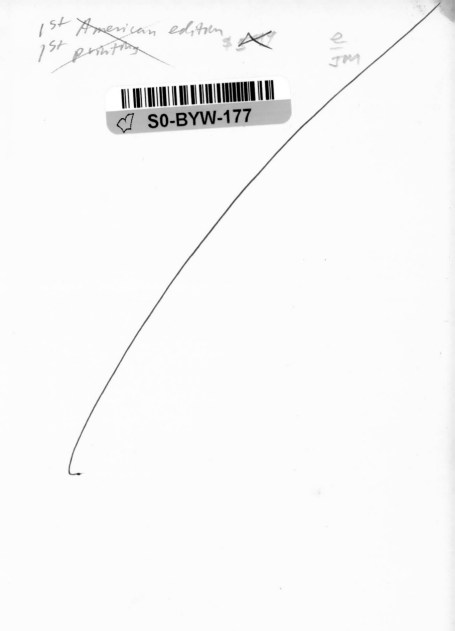

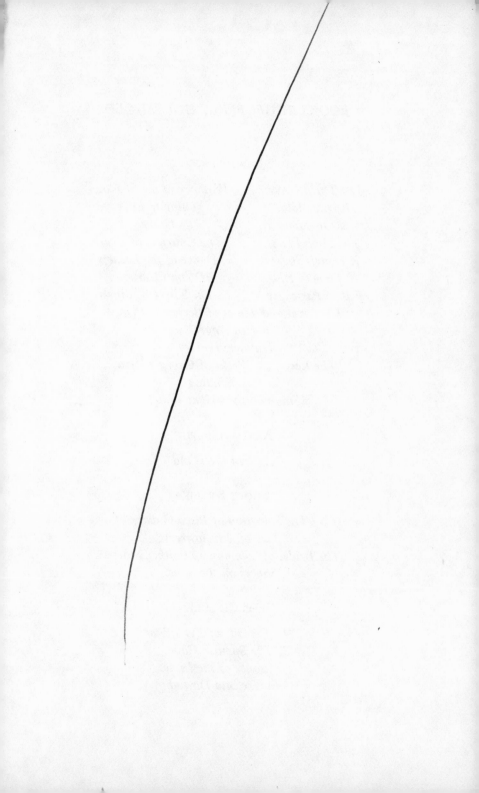

## BOOKS BY GEOFFREY HOUSEHOLD

### NOVELS

| | |
|---|---|
| *The Third Hour* | *Watcher in the Shadows* |
| *Rogue Male* | *Thing to Love* |
| *Arabesque* | *Olura* |
| *The High Place* | *The Courtesy of Death* |
| *A Rough Shoot* | *Dance of the Dwarfs* |
| *A Time to Kill* | *Doom's Caravan* |
| *Fellow Passenger* | *The Three Sentinels* |

*The Lives and Times of Bernardo Brown*
*Red Anger*
*Hostage: London*
*The Last Two Weeks of Georges Rivac*
*The Sending*
*Summon the Bright Water*

### AUTOBIOGRAPHY

*Against the Wind*

### SHORT STORIES

*The Salvation of Pisco Gabar*
*Tale of Adventurers*
*The Brides of Solomon and Other Stories*
*Sabres on the Sand*

### FOR CHILDREN

*The Exploits of Xenophon*
*The Spanish Cave*
*Prisoner of the Indies*
*Escape into Daylight*

# SUMMON THE
# BRIGHT WATER

# SUMMON THE BRIGHT WATER

## GEOFFREY HOUSEHOLD

*AN ATLANTIC MONTHLY PRESS BOOK*
LITTLE, BROWN AND COMPANY  BOSTON/TORONTO

FIRST AMERICAN EDITION

*Library of Congress Cataloging in Publication Data*

Household, Geoffrey, 1900–
Summon the bright water

"An Atlantic Monthly Press book."
I. Title.
PR6015.07885S9 1981   823'.912   81-8171
ISBN 0-316-37439-3                 AACR2

ATLANTIC-LITTLE, BROWN BOOKS
ARE PUBLISHED BY
LITTLE, BROWN AND COMPANY
IN ASSOCIATION WITH
THE ATLANTIC MONTHLY PRESS

BP

Designed by Janis Capone

*Published simultaneously in Canada
by Little, Brown & Company (Canada) Limited*

PRINTED IN THE UNITED STATES OF AMERICA

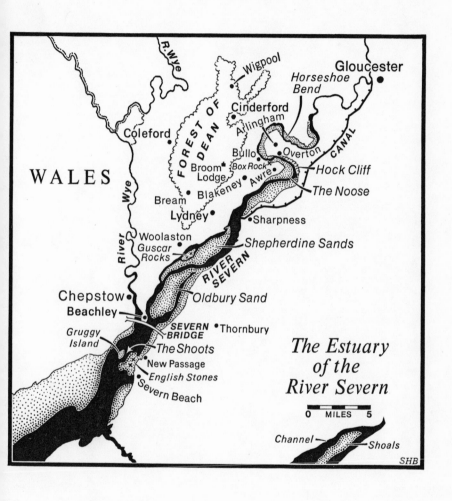

The Estuary
of the
River Severn

*PART*

II

have returned. Now that the Forest has again closed over me I feel that I am welcome, that under the dense mysteries of vegetation must be the answer — well, not the answer but a readiness to sense what it should be. One cannot live here without the genes of far-distant ancestors responding. I see in myself some resemblance to a werewolf. When I have to appear by day I am a good and reputable citizen whose name is not unknown in learned circles; by night I am a prowler under the oaks determined to find out why I was worth killing. Why was I so important? Which of his precious secrets, mostly bogus but one undeniably solid, did he suspect I might discover?

And discover where it is, what is its date and what its source I will. Meanwhile I wish to prepare a record of events which will explain my own actions and serve as the basis of my defense if I am run in on a charge of murder and, perhaps, of burglary.

When I was safely on the bank after the fight with the Severn for my life and wondering why Simeon Marrin should have encouraged me in what he must have known was sheer suicide I remembered having told him that nobody knew where I was. So it was safe to kill me. But instead of storming back to him in justifiable fury I chose to remain dead. That decision — so far as I can analyze myself in this dark shelter of dead twigs and broken brick, to which I have now returned, was due to indignant curiosity. I had a better chance of discovering the truth if I didn't exist.

My dear policeman, if my movements begin to demand investigation — unlikely, but one never knows — no doubt you will first inquire how I earn my living and will be told that I am an economic historian. My specialty is the study of ancient economies. That is a sideline which will not interest you. It should, and I will go into it later at more length.

The first cause of my being in the Forest of Dean when I was supposed to be in Spain is sheer exasperation. I was about to fly to Seville. When the plane was ready to take off one engine started to flame. The aircraft was removed to the workshops and the passengers to a foul hotel of computerized luxury. Most of the following day was spent fuming in the passenger lounges of Heathrow. In the evening we were told with the usual self-righteousness that the flight was canceled and that another night would have to be spent at that imperial caravansary of the damned. I cleared out and returned to my apartment. Instead of exploring the banks of the Guadalquivir, decently dressed and equipped, I decided to explore those of the Severn in marching order with a pack on my back, my feet being more reliable than airline timetables. I had long wanted to see for myself whether there was any possible site for a Roman port on the east bank of the estuary, though I did not intend a serious investigation, only a solitary, enjoyable walk with a good excuse for it.

And so, you see, if by bad luck you have become interested in the name of Piers Colet, all his friends will have told you he is in Seville. I must admit it looks like meticulous planning, but it was not.

As you know — or would know if you belonged to the Gloucester or Bristol police — the roads on the east of the Severn Sea are for the most part a mile or two away from the water and little can be seen but the meadows and the seawall. The only way to carry out a close examination of the sands and channels is to walk along the embankment until you are stopped by a muddy pill — as

Gloucestershire calls the outlet of a stream — to strike back to the nearest bridge, jumping or failing to jump the drainage ditches, and then return to the estuary and repeat the process. On the face of it a boat would seem more practical, but the channels are not easy. Set out on the flood after the Severn bore has passed upriver, and you will see no more than a full and swirling estuary. To the eye it is as majestic as the great seaway of the Thames, yet there may be less than a fathom of water under the keel, and it is said to be possible — though not advisable — to walk across from bank to bank at low tide and stay dry above the knees.

No, the only course for a historian seeking a worked block of stone which might once have belonged to a quay is to walk, to wade and to call for advice at a village pub or the isolated cottage of a salmon fisherman. I have no doubt that navigation was just as tricky two thousand years ago, let alone the fact that a port on the east bank would have served no known purpose.

After crossing the Severn Bridge I spent the night at Beachley and next day started up the west bank where Romans loaded the iron from the Forest of Dean in their ports of Woolaston and Lydney, already well known and partly excavated. So I was more sightseer than explorer, but again I left the road to follow the river where it was possible. That was not often, for the lanes down to the tideway are few and the embankment is pierced by deeper pills than on the east bank, fed by streams running down from the dark line of the Forest.

Outside Blakeney, when I must have covered all of twenty miles, I stopped at a pub and drank a pint of excellent perry, tempted to try this product of the orchards of ancient pear trees between the road and the Severn. The pub did not let rooms and I asked the landlord if he could recommend anywhere else, not too far away, where I could stay the night. True disaster can only spring from such natural questions which lead so innocently to the unforeseen. I wish to God I had never asked that question. Well do I? If I hadn't I should never have met Elsa.

"There's the guesthouse at Broom Lodge," he replied. I detected a slight note of doubt in his voice. It married with my own doubts. I do not like places called guesthouses. The food is usually awful and the proprietor either discourteous or painfully hearty.

"What's it like?" I asked.

"It's a farm," he said. "Communist they calls it."

"Communal, Dad," his daughter corrected him.

"Aye. Sort of monastery, like. And they run a guesthouse where anyone is welcome if he's presentable."

"A Catholic monastery?"

"Not they. Not church nor chapel neither. But I hear it's bloody religious one way or another."

It sounded as if it might be a refuge for some crazy Christian sect or Zen Buddhists or one of the offshoots of Hinduism involving meditation and milk, but my curiosity was aroused. I am always eager to understand how a commune of inefficient farmers can produce enough food to feed themselves and their families. The usual answer is that they can't, and consequently return to the rat race. But when they can, an analysis of their organization often has something to teach us of the past and possible future.

The landlord gave me exact directions for a shortcut to Broom Lodge. After a mile of road through scattered cottages, never grouped into anything one could call a village, I came to a green bridle path through the Forest. The great oaks shut out most of the sky and all the activities, themselves silent enough, of the grasslands. There was no undergrowth but the miniature jungle of young shoots of bracken, from which sheep once appeared and crossed the path, apparently unattended and unconfined by any fence.

Reaching a road, I turned left as directed and arrived at the drive leading to Broom Lodge. It was a long, white house of two stories built in the early nineteenth century, with many modern outbuildings, and shut in by the Forest on three sides. The front faced open country to the southwest and commanded a distant view across the river to Sharpness Docks, where little ships bound for Gloucester thankfully abandoned the estuary and entered a canal.

There was no one about but a young man who was digging up

the tulips and putting in bedding plants. He was very pink and white, bare to the waist of his muddy corduroy trousers, and did not look as if gardening were his normal task. His clean-shaven, demure face and unsteady blue eyes suggested a curate attending to the vicarage garden. When I told him I had heard that travelers could be put up for the night, he agreed fervently that they could. Yes, yes they could. Indeed they could. Someone would come out shortly to receive me. At the moment the management was in conference.

This unexpected echo from the commercial world amused me; it also suggested that here might be a commune efficiently run. A homemade bench of oak on the well-kept lawn faced the front door and there I sat waiting for the religion to turn up.

It came out, slender, tall and commanding. She looked just right for an abbess in spite of sweater and slacks, with large eyes and a full-lipped mouth in a serene oval face. She might, I thought, lack piety, but not discipline.

I introduced myself, explaining that I was on a walking tour of the tidal Severn and so had no more baggage than the small pack on my back. She was kind enough to say that I was just the sort of person they liked to entertain, and led me off to a recently built annex extending from the main house into the Forest to show me the accommodation.

It was simple: a whitewashed cell with a comfortable bed, a table and an armchair. There were four or five other cells opening out of the passage, and at the end of it a fine, tiled washroom with showers and lavatories. She hoped I would join the community for supper. I should come along to the bar when I was ready.

I was glad to hear that there was a bar. The atmosphere of mixed simplicity and affluence puzzled me. It did not fit the pattern of a large farm which ran a guesthouse on the side. Monastic rule must come in somewhere. Indeed I might have dropped in at a medieval abbey famed for its hospitality. The handsome young abbess had mentioned no charge for bed and breakfast.

Having made myself as presentable as I could, I returned to the entrance hall of the main building. Double doors wide open gave me a sight of the refectory arranged like a school or college dining hall with a high table and two short wings. Across the way was the so-called bar, which more resembled a small party in a country house with the host serving drinks from a white-clothed sideboard and his guests scattered about. The abbess, who had changed into a black robe with a curiously heavy gold brooch beneath one shoulder, came forward to greet me and led me to the dispenser of alcohol and wisdom.

"This is my uncle, Simeon Marrin, and this is Major Denzil Matravers-Drummond, another of our guests."

This first meeting with Marrin failed to give me any clear impression of the man. Tall and thin but with chest and arms well developed he could have been a somewhat ascetic clergyman in his forties who, say, had rowed for his college in youth. His gray eyes were large and far apart, like those of his niece though not as calm. Power, yes. I cannot be sure, but I think I sensed that. In any case it was not long before I did.

The major was of a very different species, older, preoccupied and with a nervous trick of raising his hand to pull at a mustache which no longer existed. One could hazard a guess that like many retired military men he was busy catching up with obscure intellectual interests — a likely type to fall for whatever Broom Lodgism was. The odd score of colonists sitting or standing about the room were mostly young men and women, healthy and attractive. But among them was a minority who fitted my expectations, satisfied with their own salvation and looking as if they had just returned from a psychiatrist who had successfully excised another piece of individual character. It seemed odd that all these were bald.

We trooped in to supper. I had been placed between Simeon Marrin and his niece Elsa. On Marrin's other side was the major who, I gathered, had visited Broom Lodge on several occasions. The rule seemed to be that one stiff drink or a sherry was permissible before the meal. At table one was offered a soft drink or a mug of cider or perry from the Severnside orchards.

"How did you hear of us, Mr. Colet?" Marrin asked.

"From the landlord of the inn at Blakeney."

I told him how I had been walking down the left bank and up the right bank of the Severn Sea with a vague interest in Roman ports.

"Are you an archaeologist?" Elsa asked.

"No, an economist specializing in ancient history. Archaeologists find and uncover the buildings. I want to know how the people who lived in them had enough to eat."

"Ah! Ancient agriculture, what!" the major exclaimed. "Just the man for you, Simeon! Now, Mr. Colet, tell us how the Egyptians could afford to take such a mass of labor off the land to build pyramids and still feed the people. What?"

Such an invitation to talk inevitably made me commit the crime of lecturing at dinner. I addressed myself mostly to Elsa and not only from curiosity. When she was interested her face lit up and I realized for the first time that she was extremely attractive. As a concession to the formality of the evening meal she had let loose the ash-blonde hair which when I first saw her had been coiled in a severe bun.

So I replied that the major was right in supposing that one of my subjects was subsistence agriculture. For example, I could understand how such a commune as Broom Lodge just managed to feed its colonists, but I should be fascinated to learn how it produced surplus value, as it obviously did.

"I will show you around tomorrow, Mr. Colet," Marrin said.

The subject was promptly dropped. Elsa broke the respectful silence by asking about Roman ports on the Severn. I explained that on the east bank there were apparently none. If one were found it might suggest new aspects of the imperial economy: transport of slaves and rations, for example. The ports on the west bank represented straightforward capitalism — mining of iron in the Forest of Dean and direct shipment to the Continent.

"Some say gold, too," the major remarked. He bent forward across Marrin as if eagerly waiting a reply.

"A tradition with no truth in it," Marrin interrupted. "Geologically it is most unlikely. But that hasn't stopped prospectors from searching for it from time to time."

I look back now at the first mention of gold. The thread of gold runs through the mysterious tapestry of Broom Lodge. I see it again and again appearing on the surface but still forming no recognizable or believable design.

My first impression of the colonists was that they were a hardworking bunch, starry-eyed or not, who knew the figures for profit and loss on their various enterprises but seemed vague about those for the whole commune. Pigs were the mainstay. Broom Lodge had ancient and extensive rights of common in the Forest, and the pigs were free to wander and stuff themselves with acorns in season. Superior flavor had won the colonists a London market for the products of the smokehouse. They were also breeding back to the wild boar since there was a demand, chiefly from the Continent, for its meat.

However, the pigs, a flock of sheep — also benefiting from common rights — and a hundred acres of arable land could not possibly give a return to keep some thirty men and women living in civilized comfort. By the time I was off to an early bed it was obvious to me that Simeon Marrin was subsidizing the colony from income or capital. Why? The propagation of his gospel, whatever it was, had to be the answer.

In the morning, walking around the estate with him, I saw that his hospitality must be even more generous than I had supposed. The commune turned out to be a training center, and the training was nothing like so efficient as the farming. We started off in the wheelwright's shop where two married couples were hard at work on wagon wheels and more delicate jobs for dogcarts and buggies. They must have had some practical lessons elsewhere but now were following drawings and diagrams. A finished wheel, though smartly painted and with professional slender spokes, was to my eyes very slightly oval.

The next call was at the smithy. Four of the bald men were forging simple tools and wrought iron. I looked more closely at them and saw that they were tonsured. Then we came to a carpenter's shop with a primitive lathe worked by pedals. There two colonists were also tonsured. Still another was the young gardener who had received me on arrival, making seven in all.

Last was a sailmaker's loft where three women were stitching away. I was not able to judge their mastery of the craft, but I couldn't help remarking that the Severn seemed the last place for a carefree yachting holiday.

"Man sets out upon great waters, Mr. Colet," Marrin said in a priestly tone.

"But all these things you could buy well under the cost of home production."

"It is of course a waste of labor which should be employed on the land; but to be self-supporting is not the only object of my colony."

My colony. Not our colony. Well, that was what I suspected. He financed Broom Lodge and almost certainly owned it.

"And the other object?" I asked.

"A certain continuity. I feel that as a researcher into the past of mankind you may possibly understand our planning for the future."

That sounded as if Broom Lodge were more concerned with bodies than souls and I was prepared to listen. A future in which small communities feed themselves while the silicon chip does the rest is at least worth analysis for fun.

"Do you, I wonder, agree with us that our civilization is doomed?"

"Not in the near future."

"Near or far does not matter, for after death there is no more time. And reincarnation, do you believe in that?"

"I put it among the more improbable possibilities."

"But not impossible?"

I replied that nothing was impossible, that our ignorance was complete and had to be.

"Not complete. All of us here remember something of past lives."

An ancient and venerated faith. It seemed reasonable cement for holding together a community of believers.

"Past lives — they always seem so suspiciously romantic."

"We are aware of that, Mr. Colet. The human mind must be allowed its little vanities. What matters is the memory of service, conscious or unconscious. I will give you a hypothetical example from yourself. Let us say that you were a quantity surveyor — as we should now call it — at Tyre. You were able to tell the merchants what it would cost to build the causeway joining the island to the mainland and on your estimate they could base their decision. You remember nothing of it, but your interest in the economy of ancient harbors remains."

Right up my alley! But I doubt if the trade figures for Tyre can even be conjectured. However, it would be an amusing exercise for a wet Sunday afternoon.

It was a brilliant example of what he meant, and I told him so. As intimacy was growing, I ventured to ask him what service he himself remembered. "It may have been I who discovered that the gold which oozed from nuggets in the fire could be made to take any shape the craftsman wished. Or it may be that the liquid gold, easiest of metals, led me to try the smelting of copper and tin. I cannot be sure and it is not important. Our first belief is in reincarnation. Our second is that service to man is what is remembered. Our third is that we must prepare for such service."

I objected that if, say, an expert in genetic engineering were to be reincarnated with his memory of service it would be only a nightmare when the technology to use his science didn't exist.

"That is why we stick to the most primitive crafts — the wheel, the lathe, the sail and the working of gold."

That was a craft I had not been shown. I took him to be quite sincere. I now know that he is not only sincere but fanatically possessed. Murder for the sake of religion has never been a problem for the fanatic. Look at Hindu and Mohammedan in India or the bloodthirsty sects of the Middle East or, nearer to our own cultural aberrations, that fellow Jones who fascinated his entire colony in Guyana into committing suicide.

"You envisage that sooner or later we are bound to return to a Neolithic era?"

"Exactly. As Einstein said, the Fourth World War will be fought with stones and clubs. Then it is time for the teachers of agriculture and worship who later are remembered as gods. We are training to be those gods."

A shattering conception! But given the highly dubious premises, the conclusion follows. I wanted to ask him about the worship, but before I could do so he said very cordially:

"Stay with us as long as you like. My niece and I will be delighted."

I thanked him and replied that I would indeed like to see more of their commune. Both of them had a disturbing charm, disturbing because it defied analysis. Elsa, I found, always wore the black robe when on her many duties in the house. The sweater and slacks in which I had first seen her were for farm and garden.

That afternoon and evening, helping to turn the hay and mixing with the colonists afterward, I encouraged them to consider me as a possible convert and to talk freely. All the details of their bizarre faith are irrelevant to my narrative. Mostly they seemed fairly orthodox theosophists, speaking of the body as a temporary illusion. Meanwhile the illusion worked nobly at filling wheelbarrows with unsuitable clay for making bricks.

This core of solid Englishmen and a few women greatly respected Simeon Marrin. The Freedom of the Forest meant to them something more than the ancient rights of free miners and of shepherds who owned flocks but no land. It was as if this outpost of the oaks between the Severn and the Welsh Marshes formed for them a spiritual island where the inexorable Wheel — a pleasanter name than the rat race — forgot to turn, and left body and soul at peace with each other. One of the busy haymakers put it very well. "I love the Forest," he said. "I would like to become a tree." I don't know whether adepts of theosophy consider a tree as a possible stopping place on the way up or down, but now that the trees share my bed in silence and without eyes see from the topmost branches moonlight on the shoals of the Severn I appreciate what he meant.

Besides these honest colonists who found a spiritual peace among the oaks without worrying overmuch about past and future lives there was this inner circle of tonsured mystics. They had a courteous habit of inclining their heads whenever they met Marrin and he acknowledged their bows gravely as a high priest among his people. Nobody commented on this, accepting that they had an arcane reason of their own for such respect. I was told that they followed a tradition which descended from the Druids, who also believed in the transmigration of souls. I wish that Roman historians could have told us how the doctrine traveled from the East to the mists of the Atlantic.

After dinner Marrin took me to his own quarters at the back of the western wing where he had a formal estate office on the ground floor and above it a workshop which was far from formal and was approached by open stairs from the office. It was a circular room, contained in a squat but imposing tower, with windows high up in the wall. In the center was an electric furnace and a long laboratory table with a number of crucibles and all the usual equipment. Cabinets held a range of cream-colored ceramic pots, each marked with its chemical symbol. I noticed mercury, lead and sulfur. There were skeletons of a large salmon and a small Severn-caught dolphin. A third skeleton, standing on its own pedestal, was of some four-footed, long-tailed beast, covered with a carapace. I guessed that it was a species of turtle. The whole display was slightly theatrical. I mentioned that his laboratory resembled an alchemist's den.

"I know it does," he replied, "but that is inevitable when I am experimenting with gold and its alloys. Also I am studying the development of life in the water and all its implications. The tideway of the Severn has much to offer the mystic, from the lamprey, most primitive of fish, to the leaping, splendid salmon and the muscles of its tail."

"And the turtle," I asked, "if it is one?"

"Oh he was put in for fun! Since the place looked like a alchemist's den, as you called it, I made a proper job of the decorations."

Much later, when I was puzzled by the gold and its origin, it occurred to me that there was no better disguise for the alchemist than admitting to a stranger that he amused himself by pretending to be one.

He opened a velvet-lined drawer and showed me some of his work: bracelets, pendants and ashtrays like little scallop shells which were delicate enough for the butt ends of a millionairess. He had a genius for pure form rather than decoration. When I praised his simple and effective taste, he obviously thought that I had chosen the right words and was pleased.

"Form!" he said. "Yes, form is essential for craftsmanship but not enough. There must also be inspiration."

He hesitated and then added almost reluctantly:

"Mr. Colet, I cannot resist showing you what I mean."

I had noticed that between two of the windows was a short crimson curtain over a curved shelf. He pulled a string which drew back the curtain and exposed a casket of ebony and ivory with both the Cross and the Pentacle — an odd combination — engraved on the door. He drew a key from his pocket and unlocked the casket, revealing a two-handled vessel of gold. I had never seen anything like it, nor could I guess its function. It was too tall for an amphora or bowl and most resembled a cauldron, swelling out from the base and in again to a slight neck above the handles and below the rim. It stood about a foot high, with its smooth womb a little less. The curves of pure gold seemed to provide their own light and were as near perfection as any Chinese masterpiece of jade or porcelain. Since it was well above eye level I could not judge its weight, but felt sure he was justified in claiming to be inspired — certainly by some ancient style.

I had only time to exclaim my admiration before he shut and locked the casket, closing as it were all further comment. I didn't attempt any. I came down to earth and asked him if he had a market for such pieces.

"Yes. Every so often I go up to London with my wares and sell them. If buyers do not think them salable they can always melt them down."

In that case he could not make a profit after buying his gold, but I gave the question no further thought. Profit was of no importance if he was only training himself and preparing a memory which, according to him, would be preserved from one existence to another. An absurd faith, but no madder than some. At least it was service which was remembered, not the erotic adventures of some Oriental princess.

Verging on comedy rather than mystery was the spiritual pilgrimage of Major Matravers-Drummond. Since he was the only other guest and his room was next door to mine we were able to relax together at the day's end with his private bottle of whisky. He was Gloucestershire born and bred with his home in a valley of the dark line of the Cotswolds, which closed the eastern horizon across the river. Retired from the Household Cavalry he had taken to religion and even entered a seminary to be trained as a parson.

"Threw me out, Piers! Quite right too! My view of eternity was too far from the Book of Revelations."

"But what are you doing in this nest of reincarnationists when you are an earnest Christian?" I asked.

"I search, old boy. Look on me as a wandering friar! If Simeon chooses to believe that he is training to be a human god, I don't argue. At bottom he and his disciples long for ways of life that have been lost. No harm in that. I do myself. Started as a child. Something in me is still a British Roman of the Age of Arthur, watching Christianity and civilization collapse around him."

I could understand that. Brought up on those rich and gentle hills, surrounded by the shards of Roman villas and traveling still by Roman roads, an obsession with the farming, the fighting and the decaying towns at the end of the Empire was natural enough.

"And you think that collapse will come again?"

"If it is the will of God. All I feel is great sympathy with the past, which might be memory."

As bad as the rest of them, I thought. He's going to tell me that he rode with Arthur's cavalry, which smashed the Saxons at Badon and became — though no one knows why — a legend.

"And what were you?"

"I am. That's all. No beginnings, no ends. After death one is present both in past and future. Sometimes in life too!"

A bold and compassionate man he turned out to be, but at that first intimate chat with him I feared he was too preoccupied with the violence of his former profession and more likely to have been a carrion crow than a proconsul. He had no patience with the druidical dropouts who showed such exaggerated respect for Marrin.

"Druids! Pah!" he snorted. "You say you've seen his golden chalice. What do you think of it?"

"Remarkable workmanship."

"Blasphemy — that's what I think of it! Some of those chaps believe that Simeon has remade the Grail!"

I couldn't at first see what he meant. If the Grail ever existed, it couldn't be remade. But yes, he said, it could. It was the holiest symbol of Christianity after the Cross. Its spiritual meaning was eternal. Its physical form could be fashioned again and again.

"I suspect those fellows use it in vile heathen rites," he exclaimed.

My Arthurian major was of course tempted to dream of Marrin's cauldron as the Grail, but it seemed to me that his logic was just as fantastic. If the Grail was an eternal symbol of human longing, the heathen could benefit from its power as well as anyone else. For the first time it occurred to me — then only as a flight of fancy — that the cauldron could be older than the traditional Grail and the memory of it perhaps the origin of the myth. In that case Marrin had not made it, but found it.

I stayed on at Broom Lodge. My interest was not only in subsistence agriculture and monastic industry. I dislike writing of the other interest, for details would be in the worst taste if they became public. But this confession is for the police, should it ever be necessary for me to defend myself. Otherwise, it will be seen only by the red squirrel which has discovered me and suspects that I

17 ]

turn over the white leaves of my notebook to look for nuts. He at least will forgive me if I show my delight in love under the oaks.

I think that other guests at Broom Lodge must have been intimidated by the abbess or in a hurry to get away or, like the major, too perplexed by the past in the present and the future in the past. I am not, I know, particularly attractive to women. I have a narrow, thin-lipped, dark face and a lean body hardened by travel in search of evidence that archaeologists are too busy with tombs and temples to discover. I have also a lean mind which fails to notice birthdays, moods, hair and other surface femininities when deeply engaged in what has been called dream statistics: a fair description though intended to hurt. So I was surprised to notice — some things I do notice — that Elsa was unmistakably trying to draw attention to herself and, like an awkward young girl, interrupting conversations.

"You must come and see the mines," she said to me on the third afternoon.

The main collieries of the Forest are abandoned, leaving remarkably little industrial mess behind. The seams were rich and there was no gas but, as the shafts deepened, the costs and difficulties of pumping out the water became prohibitive. The shape of the Forest is an irregular crater not at all obvious to the eye among sharply contoured wooded hillocks but pulling into itself any stream on its way to the Severn.

Free mines, however, are still worked and anywhere in a clearing you may come upon a syndicate of two or three exploiting their shallow shaft with pick, shovel and a little railroad to the surface. Dells and hollows which seem a pleasant freak of nature were once mines, some of them worked by Celt and Roman for iron, before it was discovered that the black rock close to the surface would burn.

I had thought it was an abandoned pit which Elsa wanted me to see; but, as we walked along the green bridle path into the heart of the Forest chatting of nothing and aware of everything, she in that attractive black robe hanging prettily straight from the shoulder and chastely outlining high breasts and long legs, she turned aside several times to show me hidden depressions where the bracken gave way to wildflowers and coarse grass and glimpses of bare rock. At last she settled down in one of these pastoral hollows, a dancing ground for nymphs.

"I come here when I am tired of that Broom Lodge," she said, patting the slope of grass as an invitation to join her.

I was surprised. I had taken her to be as wholehearted an enthusiast as her uncle. I remarked cautiously that perhaps it was all a bit too solemn.

"There hasn't been an Elsa before and there won't be an Elsa again," she exclaimed.

To this petulance I answered boldly that for her very individual loveliness it could be true.

"You know perfectly well what I meant!"

"So do you — what *I* meant."

"Am I 'maternal'?" She put the word in quotation marks.

"I don't know. If you don't feel maternal you play it very well."

She did. There were of course no servants at Broom Lodge. Everything was done by the colonists themselves according to their abilities. For example, those who could cook took turns at it. But somebody had to keep an eye on the housekeeping and general organization, and that was Elsa's job.

"Of course I do. They all trust me, and Simeon has no time for little things. He has done so much. We were very poor to start with."

She went on to say that I should not misunderstand her. She loved the commune and believed it was the right way to live.

"But the religion?" I suggested.

"Well, why should I spoil it for them? But my body is *not* an illusion, damn it!"

Again the touch of little girl. I waited for more.

"And I'm too tall for them."

Members of the commune were of average height, but she and her uncle — Elsa nearly six feet and he rather more — seemed to tower over them. That effect was due to their air of kindly authority rather than the slight differences of inches.

With a sudden movement she uncoiled and got up. I did so, too, but less gracefully. When we stood facing each other her gray eyes were on a level with mine. It was impossible to look over them and I did not want to look away from them. As four eyes so ignored the space between them, there might as well be none. I pulled her to me and kissed her. Her response showed that it was what she expected. She may have persuaded herself that standing up she was less committed.

"They are all . . . Oh, for them I might come from another world!" she exclaimed.

"Sit down and tell me about it."

"I shan't tell you about it. It's just that I hate it. I feel they think it's wrong to touch me."

Myself I felt it was a sin not to. Her voice and expression implied that "they" didn't entirely resist temptation but then snatched hands back from the fire so that affairs tended to be exasperating and awkward. She was now sitting close to me and her head dreamily tilted back offered her mouth again. She made no effort to stop that severe robe from slipping away and then was tremulous but without protest as kisses wandered far and wide until both of us were overwhelmed by that unforgettable demand which still falls short of love but is far more beautiful than crude passion.

"That was rape," she whispered with pretended indignation.

Her face was turned away, but one arm was flung out asking to be adored. Of all the erogenous zones a cool, slender arm is to me the most alluring, for it is so lightly joined to all the rest that it seems to be in control of its own movements and has its own personality: I raped that too — in reality now, for I do not think it had experienced such desire before. Its owner was jealous. This time she was surprised at the response of her body, that illusion, and clung to me as if I were life itself.

"How old do you think I am?" she asked.

"In your twenties somewhere."

To be honest I would have put her in her early thirties and at the very prime of her authority and beauty.

"I am twenty-two."

"And you are really Simeon's niece?"

"Of course I am."

She told me how it had all started when she had left school and had begun a course in hotel management. Both her parents had died young and she lived with her grandmother, a vaguely kind woman occupied with good works and giving little companionship. In that dull homelife the visits of Uncle Simeon, her father's brother, had been the only bright spots for her. He was always a mysterious and stimulating character earning his living as a laboratory technician and spending his evenings with what he called The Fellowship. Several times he had taken her with him to their meetings in a barren little hall. Their principles had been easy enough to understand but quite unbelievable for a girl bursting to accept with joy whatever the present life was about to offer. He had given her books to read and she had dutifully read them, though rejecting all the arguments after the first chapter. She avoided telling him so outright since she was grateful for his interest in her.

Broom Lodge had been left to The Fellowship by one of its corresponding members, a retired clergyman who had lived there for years in an atmosphere of heresy and squalor which bothered nobody but himself. His will proposed that it should be used as a country home for the faithful — a thoroughly impractical legacy since none of them could find the money to repair and maintain the place or to restore some value to the neglected land. Simeon, however, had jumped at the opportunity and with fire and faith had persuaded half a dozen of The Fellowship not to sell it but to try their hands at a working commune where all believers would be welcome. Elsa of course must come along. She finished half her course and joined them.

It was still hell, she said, when she arrived there, and if it had not been that she fell in love with the Forest and was flattered to know herself of real service to these industrious innocents — all of whom were almost double her age or near it — she would have cleared out. Simeon himself had been tireless, she said. The two local skills by which a little money might be made were mining and salmon fishing. Broom Lodge had no rights to mine but anyone was free to catch salmon in the estuary away from the bank. The expertise of the few remaining professionals with their lave nets, weirs and stopping boats could never be acquired, so Simeon decided to try the unprecedented technique of skin diving, one of his many pseudoscientific accomplishments, half mystical, half very real.

"In the Severn? My God!" I exclaimed.

"Oh, he says it's quite safe once you know the channels and the tides. He often does it still, but at night."

"Has he ever caught anything?"

"Nothing much. But he once speared a dolphin — the one you saw in his laboratory."

The change in Broom Lodge was a year old. Along with the builders and the tractors came the workshops and recruiting of more of the faithful. Simeon had had a big win on the football pools and devoted the lot to his commune. The new intake of devout colonists had to be impressed by more than height and competence, and that was why Elsa had invented a uniform for herself, halfway between a parlormaid and a nun. It seemed so absurd to flaunt color at them when all they wanted — usually — was a mother figure.

We agreed that no one must suspect our affair. Uncle Simeon, she thought, might be sympathetic but would not approve of so swift an attachment to a stranger. As for the colonists, whatever image they had of her — abbess, housekeeper or serene, maternal beauty — would be severely dented.

Enough of Elsa for the moment — though I can never have enough. We returned in time for the hour of meditation, which out of courtesy to my hosts I attended. For me meditation is more peaceful and productive after half a liter of claret and a square meal, but on this occasion I had plenty to meditate about: whether I could save myself from falling desperately in love with Elsa and how much to believe of the story of the win of the pools. It neatly accounted for the comfort of Broom Lodge, which had puzzled me, as well as for the unproductive farming and the impossibility of any large profits on Marrin's buying and selling of gold; all the same, he was not the sort of character to study football results and to waste time and money on a weekly gamble. Of course he might have done it once only and produced a winning line by following some incredibly effective cabalistic formula, but a pious and profitable burglary for the sake of the commune was far more likely.

By the time the party broke up with a monotonous chant my thoughts had switched to salmon fishing, Marrin's early and wildly imaginative scheme to raise some cash. Since I myself am a competent skin diver, I was eager to talk to him about the risks of the Severn Sea and the possibilities of underwater exploration.

First, I engaged the major in conversation on the founding of the colony, so that there could be no reason to suspect Elsa of giving the story away. He avoided any discussion of the win on the pools, saying that there were many unexpected ways in which the spiritually minded could be rewarded. When I suggested that the acquisition of worldly wealth was usually supposed to distract the Soul from the Way, he did not agree. Poverty was desirable for the monk but not for the monastery. This led quite naturally to the early skin diving for profit. Later on, the major said, it had become a rite. Marrin's secret swimming with the fish was symbolic of the unity of life.

Symbolic, hell! A typically woolly explanation! I had little doubt that Marrin would not shrink from fraud in propagating his gospel, but in his beliefs he was sincere. As I lie here in the discomfort and physical content of any primitive pagan his doctrines seem as absurd as those of the more fantastic Christian sects. Yet one must remember that to a pious lama Broom Lodgism might seem more or less acceptable except for its emphasis on service to mankind rather than the perfecting of the soul. But that is irrelevant. The dynamic energy of a religion derives from belief, not from what is believed.

The subject came up naturally when I was discussing with

Marrin the Horseshoe Bend of the river and the Severn bore which begins there, racing up ahead of the tide like any ocean wave and leaving a full estuary behind it.

"I think I am the only person to have explored the bed," he said, "and at such a depth that I could let the bore pass over me."

I remarked in all innocence that I wished I could dive with him — but at slack water, thank you very much! He replied at once and cordially that I mustn't hope to catch salmon. I would do better to come down to the Forest next season and learn to use a lave net, spotting my salmon as it drove upstream and racing along a sandbank to intercept it.

"They always swim close to the surface," he told me. "That was where I went wrong. I had a theory that they would swim deeper where they could. So I tried the deep pools where the main channel passes close to the shore. It didn't work. But it was great joy to rest on the bottom and watch the fish passing overhead when the water was clear enough to see the streak of silver."

"But why do you go out at night?"

He hesitated, his enthusiasm gone.

"Because I found that at night I could feel as a fish feels. In the light one is only a man swimming. That is your answer!"

We were both silent for a moment; but then, apparently realizing that he had been too abrupt, he asked:

"What has been your experience underwater, Mr. Colet?"

My interest had not been in fish, but in the remains of historic ports where little remained to be seen on land — like Tyre, I said, reminding him of the quantity surveyor. Also I had accompanied a small party of prehistorians who maintained that if you wanted to study the Paleolithic you must not be content with cave dwellings by inland streams but must dive for caves now covered by the sea.

I explained that in the last Ice Age when sea levels were lower than at present, river levels must also have been lower. For example, the mouth of the Severn must have been somewhere down the Bristol Channel between woods and marshes that were now shoals; and the wide valley, where the ebb and flow of the powerful tides now played merry hell with channels and the banks, then contained a clear river of fresh water fed by the glaciers of the Welsh mountains.

"I have seen no such caves. Where would they be?"

"Beneath the ledges where Severn cliffs once stood before they were eaten back."

"All crumbled away, Mr. Colet, crumbled away to mud and sand. The Severn has no cliffs underwater."

"I think that here and there you might find a clean edge scoured by the tide if you looked at the bottom of the ebb."

"Pardon me, Mr. Colet, but you are wrong!" he exclaimed. "No sheer cliff exists."

He reminded me of one of my old tutors who, when contradicted however politely, would lean toward me chest thrust forward and head back, seeming to take up an S curve like a snake about to strike. I assumed that Marrin had visualized package tours of prehistorians or geologists come to disturb his communings with the salmon. It was from that point, I am sure, that he began to wish that I had never called in at Broom Lodge with my awkward curiosity. It was not my fault, for he had encouraged me both to ask questions and to answer them. Ancient economies interested him from two points of view: religious doom-watching and subsistence agriculture.

Our conversation left me with a feeling that Marrin considered the Severn his private property from which trespassers must be warned off. Such jealousy was quite natural; the mystical side of his night dives could be enough to account for it. But the solvency of Broom Lodge continued to puzzle me. Somewhere was deliberate deception. I had an impression — which I admitted might be due merely to his skeletons of sea creatures — that the thread of gold seemed to run out of the laboratory into the Severn and back again.

At the next chance of a private talk with Elsa I asked if her uncle had made a serious study of alchemy.

"From books, yes," she replied. "And I know he used to muck

about with experiments in the old days. But of course he didn't have a proper laboratory of his own till he could afford to build one here."

To my astonishment, Elsa who was so scornful of the beliefs of Broom Lodge had been impressed by the paraphernalia of alchemy and did not rule out the transmutation of metals. She was in good company. Isaac Newton had believed it possible and in later life suffered from fits of insanity, probably due to the ingestion of lead and mercury which he lavished on his experiments.

"Then you don't believe the football pools story?"

"Do you?"

"Well, it's possible."

"That's what I feel about the gold."

I objected that it was not possible. Gold could be made from lead but required immense and uneconomic plant — lasers and cyclotrons and God knows what. It couldn't be made by a rack of crucibles and a magic circle.

"But don't ask him about it," she warned me. "We talk of it ourselves, but never to him."

I decided that gold was none of my business; it kept this hospitable colony happy and prosperous, and the profit and loss account was a matter for the Inspector of Inland Revenue, not for me. So my thoughts returned to the trade balance of Roman Britain and its commerce. This, the original object of my wanderings, had rather faded away — not unnaturally, considering the excitement of Elsa and the surprising efficiency of Broom Lodge in spite of being collectively devoted to poppycock.

In case I revived Marrin's nightmare of prehistorians flipping in and out of his river I tackled him very cautiously. Rome seemed a safe subject, too solid, too eternally present for mysteries, and I knew he was well up to date on the long history of the Forest. So over the evening drinks I ventured to ask him if he had ever spotted any underwater foundations at Woolaston which would help archaeologists to decide whether the Romans had built a commercial wharf or just a breakwater to shelter the naval commander's galley.

His sane and pleasant side at once appeared or was allowed to appear. It may be that I have not sufficiently emphasized his personal charm, for it stands to reason; without it he could never have kept his commune together and loyal, religion or no religion.

"Why don't we both look?" he replied. "It occurs to me that we are of the same build and I have a spare suit. We'll dive in daylight, of course, and at slack water. That will be about eight to eight-thirty tomorrow, if it isn't too early for you."

It was the fourth morning of my stay. After we had grabbed a light breakfast he unlocked the door of a tiled cubicle which led off the guests' washroom at the end of the passage. There he kept his diving kit. I was glad to see that his own suit and the spare were of neoprene, for I was used to the wet suit. He had only surface life jackets but as we were unlikely to go deeper than twenty feet or so they were good enough and saved trouble.

He had chosen to go in off the Guscar Rocks, which I had never seen. The west bank of the Severn is concealed till you reach it. Rough farm tracks lead down to it from the main road to Wales and either stop at the railway embankment or go under it, always past a notice that swimming is extremely dangerous. Beyond the embankment are the flat and empty meadows, without a living thing but the sheep to take an interest in what you do or how you are equipped, abruptly ending at the immensity of the tideway, itself also empty.

It was near the time of low water and the Guscar Rocks were jagged islands of weed standing above the last eddies of the ebb. It seemed impossible to get at them, for the shore, beneath a miniature cliff of crumbling red rock, was of mud and shale; but Marrin confidently led the way along the banks of a pill until we could swim on the surface across to the rocks, land on them, and jump in from the far side clear of the weed.

The water was warmer than I expected and in spite of its color of pale milk chocolate — gold if one wants to be politer to the Severn than I feel — visibility was not too bad. All I could discover close under the Woolaston shore was that somebody at some time had built something. Not very satisfactory! A narrow and difficult secondary channel led to the old port at Lydney and may have offered a straight run upriver in Roman times. If it did, the Guscar Rocks sheltered a natural harbor. But only dredging could reveal solid evidence, and I doubt if even that expensive process would have much success against the silt and sand brought down by every relentless tide.

We pulled out again onto the rocks, facing the smooth and shining slope of gray mud and the meadows beyond. The green railway embankment, acting as a seawall, cut us off from the world of the land. Behind us the Severn was still just alive, sucking and swirling as the channel emptied the last of the ebb left behind in the backwaters of the Shepherdine Sands.

The mysterious pattern of the eddies stopped. The Severn was empty and waiting. It was time to swim ashore.

"The tide is making now," Marrin said as we took off masks and Aqualungs. "We may see the beginnings of the bore."

He had to point it out. There at Woolaston, well before the narrowing of the river, it was more a sudden rise of water level than a wave. Only the surge around the Guscar Rocks revealed the force and speed of the tide which, twenty minutes later up the Horseshoe Bend with a southwest wind behind it, would have raced on as the wave of the bore all of five feet high. Meanwhile the Shepherdine Sands, which had seemed a golden playground for children, were rippling water.

When we had crossed the embankment and our horizon again became the dark tumble of the Forest looking down across the peaceful belt farm and pasture to its incalculable estuary I suspected that the face of the Guscar rock which we had jumped from had been the top of a cliff before the rise in water level after the Ice Age. I should have remembered his resentment of prehistorians and kept speculation to myself.

"That straight edge could go down below the mud," I said, "and the chances are that the ice floes undercut it at the bottom — a useful shelter for the hunter when the climate began to warm up. Salmon by the million and the odd mammoth when he was sick of fish. With a couple of skins hanging down from the roof to keep the wind out and a good fire of driftwood he was quite as comfortable as any Canadian Indian."

"You believe that one could still find traces of such shelters?"

I replied that nobody would take the trouble to dig down through fathoms of mud just to find a hearth and some worked flints. But wherever there was a clean Severn cliff underwater the skin diver might well find some evidence that man had lived at the foot of it or under it.

"I think you were right when you told me that no such cliff remains," I added. "The only possible site would be the Shoots at the entrance to the Bristol Channel."

We drove quickly back to Broom Lodge, and after we had warmed up in hot baths he invited me up to his laboratory for a drink. There I was to see another side of him, undoubtedly more genuine than his impostures such as alchemy.

"You must have been the only person to have explored the bottom of the Severn," I said.

"In our time I may be. But long ago when, as you tell me, the sea was lower and a calm Severn flowed out to it there could have been another. You have seen the Temple of Nodens?"

I had not, though I knew of the mosaics and inscriptions.

"The god of the river and the Forest, father of Gwyn ap Nudd, prince of the underworld," Marrin said. "He was worshipped by Briton and Roman but he was here long before either of them. It might have been he who taught the forest dwellers how best to fish for salmon and how to find veins of iron and gold under the dead leaves."

"And what is he reincarnated as?" I asked. "Harbor master at Sharpness Docks?"

"That is quite possible," he answered without at all resenting my levity. "Or myself perhaps. Or just a presence of whom I am aware."

Spirits about. I was surprised; but it was to be expected. Some of the Buddhist sects do not, I believe, exclude the existence of good and evil spirits.

To change the subject I asked whether he had found his curious turtle in the Severn.

"In the deep, yes."

"You should show it to a zoologist."

"Do you know one?"

"Several. And one of them is an authority on reptiles. I'll bring him to inspect it."

It was at that point, I think, that he finally made up his mind.

"I am going to dive tomorrow night. Why not come with me? I have always wanted a companion."

"On another visit I'd like to. But I must leave tomorrow. Nobody knows where I am."

"I remember you telling me. But does nobody care, my dear Piers?" he asked, using my Christian name for the first time. "You left no address?"

"No. Letters can wait."

"And where are you going?"

"I'll have a look at your Temple of Nodens and then on into Wales."

True enough, but the real reason was that I wanted to escape. Broom Lodge, the major, Marrin himself, Elsa, and that silent and ancient Forest, so unnecessarily mysterious, were beginning to form a whole I distrusted. I needed a few days alone in which I might isolate Elsa from the rest and decide whether or not I was making a fool of myself.

"Then if you are in no hurry, come with me now! The tide will serve tomorrow night and might not on your next visit to us."

"But why not daylight?"

"Oh, you should know that! At night the strangest creatures come out of their holes and swim freely. And with a flashlight at night one sees colors as never in daylight. The kingdom of Nodens — doesn't it tempt you?"

It did. I was eager to see the glow of the weed and the silver of fish against the red and green marl of the Severn.

"Good! And may I ask you to tell no one you are going with me? Not even Elsa!"

"But why not?"

"They would be jealous and pester me until I started diving classes. You'll agree that the Severn is no place to learn. And there is another point. As between friends I can admit it to you. If they knew that I allowed you to go with me, they would see my night dives as a mere sport."

"Instead of a mystery of mysteries?"

For a moment I thought I had gone too far, but the blaze in his eyes was instantaneously extinguished. He replied quite calmly:

"To be the leader of a faith one must offer the followers secrets for their imagination as well as truth for their souls."

Never was there a more curious reason for skin diving at night, but his frankness was convincing. He himself apparently found a unity with nature in these driftings far below the swimming of the salmon. That in itself was a pleasure not far from spiritual, so in his own eyes he was justified in presenting it as an aspect of religion, perhaps linked in some way to the more dubious alchemy.

I said that I didn't see how I was to prevent the commune from knowing that I had left with him for the river.

"Oh, that's easy! Leave in the afternoon to continue your walk as you intended. At ten be on the Box Rock. You can reach it from the road to Awre. We will change there, and it is only a few yards to the ledge above my favorite deep where we will dive."

"Where can I warm up and stay the night if I don't come back to Broom Lodge?"

"Leave it to me, Piers! I'll find accommodation for you at one or other of the nearby inns and tell them to expect you late."

I felt it was absurd not to discuss his invitation with Elsa, and it is likely that I would have done so if ever we could have been together long enough for a private conversation. Neither she nor I could risk adventuring down the passages and through the main building when a party of the faithful might be meditating with open eyes, others getting up before dawn and saying good night or good morning to a prayer meeting in the hall, and the major working out Arthur's past or future tactics on the lawn. Bedroom creeping, however cautious, was out; the movements within Broom Lodge were incalculable.

So Elsa and I were limited to quick kisses in corridors with no chance to talk seriously about the future. She may have feared it and wished to avoid it. When I left in the afternoon I promised to return as soon as I decently could and meanwhile to send a letter or two to remind her of what I thought of her. She wanted to know where I would stay the night and I told her that I was going to Lydney to look at the Temple of Nodens and did not know where I should fetch up afterward — both of which were true. She insisted that I should take cider and sandwiches with me so that I could have a meal without thinking of time and communications wherever I found something worth detailed investigation.

I set off about four o'clock after telling them all how grateful I was and how interested I had been, and walked through the green forest paths to the remains of the temple set on its headland, which once must have projected into the Severn. Evidently Nodens had been one of the friendly little gods of the Celts. Marrin's suggestion that in life he had been a hero from across the seas bringing agriculture or the working of metals was a reasonable guess.

Then I took a bus up the river and walked down to the seawall where the great Horseshoe Bend begins and the tide compressed by the narrowing river explodes into the bore. I reckoned that the wave should be at its best if there was light enough to see it, for it was the night after the new moon.

I did not want to call at a pub and start eating and drinking before a dive. Marrin's deep was unlikely to be more than twenty or thirty feet at low tide, but it was bound to be tricky. However, the hours of waiting did not drag. I sat on the low red cliff above the mud watching the fearsome ebb racing down to the sea, not even sticking to the main channels of its bed but dancing in whirlpools, dashing up unseen backwaters against the flow and forming dark drifts of silt which compelled me to look up at the sky and see whether they were not the shadows of clouds overhead. But there were no clouds except over the distant Cotswold Hills when the red sun went down behind the pinnacles of the Forest leaving a warm night behind, perfect for diving.

I started to move toward the rendezvous while the long twilight could show me the way. The Box Rock ran out at a right angle to the shore and part of it was now showing above the streaming ebb. If there was a clean and sheltered drop on the downstream side it was easy to understand why Marrin had called it his favorite deep.

The first I saw of him was the pool of light from the flashlight wavering over the meadow and the offshore mud. He had his suit on under a duffel coat and carried the Aqualungs and the spare suit and life jacket for me. He helped me to dress fussily, exactly and with the utmost friendliness, meanwhile telling me of the likely conditions underwater, that I should follow him closely and that my two cylinders would allow me some eighty minutes. We should come out, however, in less than half an hour, well before the turn of the tide.

At about ten-thirty we were on the rock and ready. He walked downstream until the water was nearly up to his knees and stopped.

"We'll jump from here," he told me, "into the Box Hole. Another step and I should be over the edge of the cliff."

The dark surface of the water was disturbed for no apparent reason, I could see no other sign of a sudden increase in depth. When I jumped I fully expected to land on my bottom, but found myself easily descending along the face of rock. The tide was hardly perceptible and the water less opaque than I expected so that the colors of the Severn rock could be distinguished. Marrin kept close to me and a little ahead, his lamp showing me what to look for. Once a conger trailed out of a fissure in the cliff and passed upstream ahead of us so that one could watch the long, silver undulations, half fish and half snake. There was no weed except for occasional clumps.

When I looked for Marrin he had gone — in pursuit of the conger as I thought or perhaps out into the channel beyond the rock. Finding that I was negatively buoyant I started to walk along the bottom of the Box Hole and didn't much like it. The bottom was quicksand or some yielding emulsion of mud and sand into which the fin of my right leg sank. The effort of pulling it out broke the strap and of course drove down the left leg. Cursing Marrin for not seeing that the strap was in good condition, I recovered the fin, but it would not stay on and was useless. I pulled out the left leg with some difficulty and decided that I had had enough. The silt stirred up by my efforts blinded me and I no longer knew where the rock was. I was experienced enough not to panic, for I had only to re-lease the weight belt around my waist and come up. I didn't give a damn if his weight belt was lost forever in the sand, as it certainly would be.

I felt for the release catch but it wouldn't release; it had jammed. But it couldn't jam. Then I did panic. It had not jammed. It had been jammed — and cunningly, for I couldn't see or feel how. Meanwhile the weight of the cylinders was pushing me little by little down into the quicksand. My right leg was kicking to no purpose. My frantic efforts to clear my left leg broke the strap on that fin also.

I began to discard the lead weights from the belt, all the time sinking lower. By the time they had gone I was swallowed up to the waist. I tried to lean forward and swim like a flat fish on top of the stuff. No good. I returned or was returned to an upright posi-tion and seemed to stay there. I was not sinking anymore so long as I kept still but I could never get out. I had checked the cylinders before the start and reckoned that I had about an hour more of life before the inevitable end. It made no difference whether I chose to die by drowning or by gradual disappearance into the sand.

I might last until the arrival of the bore. That must surely finish me since the sudden increase in depth would reduce my buoyancy still further. Mental arithmetic underwater had the most curious effect of increasing rather than reducing panic until I got control of myself and was only madly impatient because I kept getting my simple sums wrong. Bottom of the ebb at the Guscar Rocks yester-day morning 8:30, and today 10:10. This evening 11. But the bottom of the ebb here should be earlier than slack water down there. Hold on! That doesn't matter to the bore. What matters is the Bristol Channel tide not the Severn which, as I had seen, can ebb backward if it likes. Bore passed the Guscar Rocks at 11. I had heard that its speed upriver was that of a galloping horse. Twelve miles it had to go. Say, fifty minutes. Bore due at 11:50. I should still have a little air left unless I had used up too much struggling with the fins. On the other hand, standing still with sand up to my chest I was using a minimum. Not that it mattered. At 11:50, give or take ten minutes, I should be dead.

I think I could never have composed my thoughts if there had been a chance of life. I was as still as a post driven into the bed of the river. The water was comfortable, its temperature cold but not too cold, possibly due to fresh water coming down from sunlit meadows. So far as movement went I was already dead, or rather in the calm of dying with the familiar objects of vision all faded away. As best I could, being an agnostic, a hopeful agnostic, I tried to concentrate on the sort of "I" which would be worthy to live without a body. The intellect, perhaps. The power to love, perhaps.

All colors darkened. The pressure on my ears was fierce and sudden. I cleared them, and then it seemed as if land and sea had dissolved into a chaos through which I was tossed and cartwheeled with no sense of position or up or down. I was conscious of speed and dreamed — so far as my brain worked at all — that it must be some limbo through which one passed at death. I never realized that the bore had passed over and taken me with it until I slammed hard into the entrance to a pill, the soft mud rising in a fountain of gobs as I hit it. The great wave, having sucked up the quicksand or forced its mass of water down into it, had carried me off along with the other debris in its path. Why I escaped I do not know. I should have gone roaring upriver surfing on the crest like a log or a drowned cow or been smashed to a sodden lump on the bottom. It might be that the weight and turbulence of water necessary to release me only operated a second or two after the crest had passed or that my near-empty cylinders were heavy enough to hold me back.

Clawing like a cat in a flower bed, I reached a low branch of hawthorn and firm ground. Upstream the young moon seemed to show plumes of spray but that may have been due to mud on my mask or grass waving in the slipstream of air. The surface of the Severn was now quite even with the tide running up behind the bore. I could imagine the silt settling, ready for the ebb to sweep it down again to the bottom of that still and deadly hole.

I did not know where I was, close to the Box Rock or a quarter of a mile upriver. The firm ground above the sharp mud valley of the pill turned out to be a little copse. I took off my harness and pushed through it, arriving at the riverside meadow where I had left my clothes. The bore had been merciful, lifting me and sweeping me around the rock.

At some time Marrin himself, while observing salmon or his soul, must have been nearly trapped in that deep chosen for my death. I don't think that he had any such intention at the Guscar Rocks though his readiness to take me along suggests that he needed to know how experienced I was and how I would react underwater in case later he should decide that I was a menace to — to what? I am still unsure. In every one of my theories there is a flaw.

My clothes were not where I had changed — he helping me, God damn him! I first assumed that Marrin had taken them back with him so as to leave no evidence. It then occurred to me that he might well require some false evidence and that he would have left my clothes on the bank in a likely place a good distance away. It would not be upstream because he would never have plunged across the pill. So it must be downstream and not far from some track, surely to be utterly deserted at night, where he had left his van. Would my clothes be in the open? Well, no. He wouldn't want them to be easily discovered by the first passerby next morning, but he wouldn't mind if they were found accidentally or by a deliberate search later on, thus muddling the date when I actually disappeared. A fairly firm beach, where I might have been tempted to have an evening swim, would be a good place. It would then be assumed that I had been caught by some whirling backwash of the ebb and drowned.

[36

My flashlight was still attached to me. I set off to walk along the bank, flashing it at intervals to see what was below: nothing at all but the swiftly rising Severn gliding past the mud. I came to the beginning of a seawall. A little way out was the top of a sand-bank which looked hard and was now separated from the land by a narrow channel and would have tempted any foolhardy inno-cent to go for a swim when the tide was low. It was easy to reach from a little beach of shale and mud immediately under the high bank, and not far away was a rutted farm track leading inland. I was sure this would have been his choice, but it took me a hell of a time to find the clothes in the dark. They were spread out above high-tide mark and hidden from the seawall itself by waving long grass.

Clearly Marrin intended that my clothes and pack should even-tually be found. It would not be known to whom they belonged since nobody would report me as missing till I failed to come home from, supposedly, Spain. It was a hundred to one against the body's ever turning up. If it did, caught in a salmon weir or bumping against a Gloucester lock, and was identified, the evi-dence of Broom Lodge would be straightforward. I had left in the afternoon. It was known that I was interested in tracing Roman ports. Yes, Marrin had lent me his diving kit. Yes, he had taken me out to the Guscar Rocks to be quite sure that I knew how to use it. The only snag was that I had not carried it when I left Broom Lodge.

I cannot guess how he intended to get out of that, unless he could persuade some members of the commune into a lie, or deny that the suit, which would be an unrecognizable rag, had ever be-longed to him. But all this is guesswork. The more I think of it, the surer I am that he was dead certain that my body could never es-cape from the bed of the river and that the question would never arise. I presume he had satisfied himself before driving away from the colony to our rendezvous with the suits and Aqualungs in the trunk that I had said nothing to Elsa.

I was nearing the limit of endurance and could now rest and re-cover Elsa's sandwiches from my pack with — thank God! — the strong Broom Lodge cider. I quickly changed and took that remote track across road and railway with the Aqualung rolled in the suit and slung from a shoulder. I was shivering in spite of the fastest walk I could manage and my only hope was to arrive soon at some quiet spot in the Forest where I could build a fire. I was instinctively against calling at the nearest house. For one thing it would have to be found. Houses are few and far between on the Severn banks. For another, Marrin was Elsa's admired uncle. But I doubt if that would have counted if I had not been obsessed by gratitude for sandwiches.

It was some two miles to the wooded slopes of the Forest. I wandered about looking for a sheltered dell and found still better cover in the tumbled entrance to a private coal mine. Vegetation had grown up around it and over the path so that I knew it was abandoned. With dead twigs and broken pit props I soon had a fire going in the entrance which could not be seen from anywhere but the immediate front.

There I warmed up and, after luxuriously dozing in the comfort, for a while returned to a shaken but more or less normal self. Imagination began to play over all those conversations with Marrin which I have recorded. Jealousy I could leave out as a motive. Elsa was really his niece, and anyway he knew nothing of our too impulsive affair.

Three clues to what had disturbed him stood out: exploration for traces of Paleolithic man; Severn cliffs; the turtle. One or all of these could reveal his carefully guarded secret of the financing of Broom Lodge. Had he found gold in some recess below the present level of the Severn? Quite impossible. Stone Age man did not know how to smelt gold or any other metal. Then could he actually be a traditional alchemist who had recovered the ritual formula for transmuting lead and mercury into gold? Nonsense! The alchemy was a smoke screen. Could he be panning some stream or sandbank in which was gold carried down from the Welsh mountains? Unlikely. It would have been discovered thousands of years before Mr. Simeon Marrin got at it. The turtle? Well, he had been evasive about the turtle, even alarmed when I talked of bringing down a zoologist to identify it. There was a connection of some sort, but not essential.

I slept at first light, wakened by the baaing of sheep when the sun was up. Stream water for breakfast. Hunger would have to wait. After scattering the ashes of my fire I set off carrying the bundle of suit and Aqualung, and strode furiously through the Forest toward Cinderford, which I assumed was big enough to possess a police station. I had no solid evidence except the weight belt — provided an expert could prove by marks that the buckle had been deliberately jammed. All the facts I could prove were that the suit was his, that he had allowed me to go to the bottom of a deep he knew was lethal and then had deserted me and kept quiet about it.

Deliberately I passed close to Broom Lodge and hid beneath the stems of a clump of foxgloves. I can only explain that by the mixture of motives inseparable from a foul temper. I wanted to see if routine was proceeding normally. I hoped to catch a glimpse of Elsa. I needed to know if Marrin had returned safely and to see his face. There was no chance of being caught unless somebody stepped on me.

Several of the druidical dropouts went off into the Forest. Useless as witnesses to anything so I let them go. The workshops were innocently busy. The only view of Elsa was her backside as she leaned over a garbage can. So I slid back into the cover of the trees, stormed on my way without caution and ran slap into the major, who was peering along a straight ash sapling he had just cut down.

"Hi! Where are you off to, Piers? I thought you had gone."

"I am off to the police station, Major, and I shall be obliged if you will come with me."

"Not going to run me in, are you?"

I didn't reply to that. My intention was to prevent him from trotting back to Broom Lodge and saying he had met me.

"Had a spot of trouble with the locals?"

I was so angry that I spat out the truth.

"Your Simeon Marrin tried to kill me last night."

"What had you found out, Piers?"

"Nothing — except that he's a fraud."

"Oh, I know that! But a prophet, possibly a prophet! So I must forgive him so long as he doesn't land himself in jail or commit unpardonable blasphemy. Don't blame you for thinking us all crackers! Simeon and the Stone Age. Me and stirrups."

"Stirrups?"

"Roman cavalry didn't have 'em in Arthur's time. Heavily armored they were. That's why folk memory called them knights when the legends started seven hundred years later. Hovered around throwing things or poking at the enemy. If you charged, either you fell off or the lance broke. Then you carried on with the spike at the other end."

Evidently the major was something of a historian. The surprise of finding that there was such a professional side to him made me forget self-pity for a moment and listen.

"Arthur's tactics — that's what I want to improve. Stirrups all they needed to be able to withdraw the lance. Then charge at the trot knee to knee and go through the Saxon infantry like a dose of salts."

"Are you proposing to alter the course of history?" I asked, for he seemed to be considering transmigration backward in time as well as forward.

"Yes. Why not? Aren't pleased with the present, are you, if you're on your way to the police station?"

He caressed his ash sapling.

"That'll be the right weight when it's seasoned," he said, "and it will bend not break. Now why set the cops on Simeon? After all he only tried to kill you. Much more important things than that! You should find out what he's up to before he can make a fool of himself again. A pity for Elsa that would be. Nice girl. Young chap like you should make a pass at her. Get your face slapped, I expect, but it won't hurt."

"Don't you know what he's up to?" I asked.

"Whatever will do the most good to the colony. Ever heard of Saint Januarius?"

"The martyr whose blood liquefies?"

[40

"That's the chap. Dried blood kept in a holy bottle of some kind. Faithful come in their thousands to see it liquefy. Priests make sure that it damn well does when it should. A lie to the senses, of course, but all to the good. It makes thousands believe truths which the senses have nothing to do with. Why are you carrying this kit? Been diving with Simeon?"

"Yes. At night this time. And over a quicksand where he knew I must drown."

"Must or could?"

"Must. But when the bore arrived it pulled up the whole bottom and me with it."

"So he doesn't know you escaped?"

"He soon will."

"Why not stay dead, old boy?"

"What for?"

"Want to know where he gets his gold from, don't you?"

"Not for myself."

"I know that. Heard you talk about a lot of antique economies on the first night. You'd rather be famous than rich every time. Stay dead and you'll have a chance. Come marching into Broom Lodge with a warrant and you won't."

I asked him what his interest was. As he had once said to me, a monk ought to live in poverty but there was no reason why the monastery should. However Marrin came by his money, it kept the commune going.

"Simple, Piers, simple! I've been worried. Old soldier. Sane sometimes. Assume Simeon made the bowl. Where did he get the gold from? Alchemy, my arse! Imagine the scandal if he's pinching it somewhere! Bloody newspaper headlines! Worse blasphemy than ever. That's what I want to avoid. Assume he scooped his bowl out of the bed of the Severn. Then did those feet in ancient time? We have to know what he has been up to. His father was a dear friend of mine. Didn't tell you that, did I? You stay dead, boy! Much more alive that way. Tuck down in the Forest somewhere near! Needn't tell me where. Two of us can check up on him when one can't."

With his visionary lunacies of Arthur, enhanced by trotting down the Mall in shining armor, his militant Christianity to match and his clipped speech he puzzled me. He must have been close on fifty, though his straight back and flat belly were those of a fit man ten years younger. But the age difference hardly counted. I realized that he was treating me as if I had been one of his trusted subalterns in trouble. There had been a wholly charming smile when he described himself as sane, sometimes.

"Stands to reason!" he went on. "You're dead and I'm not. I can't dive but I've got a car. You haven't got a car, but you can dive. I'll be in Little Drybrook outside Bream this evening with some rations. Say, half past seven. I'm a guest and don't have to dine in mess if I don't want to. Up to you whether you decide to meet me or not. Old-fashioned Humber. Black. You can't mistake it."

When I left him I was far from convinced of his reliability. But I did not go to the Cinderford police station. Marrin's motive had first to be investigated. If I could not present his reason for attempted murder my allegation might not stand up. It was open to him to swear that he had tried to rescue me, failed to find me, and in order to avoid newspaper publicity for his beloved commune had kept quiet about the accident.

To remain dead was not difficult. My name and face were only known at Beachley and Blakeney where I had stayed at inns on this side of the river. So movement was no problem, nor was food. Provided that I watched the street long enough to be sure that no member of the commune was about I could enter any village shop without arousing curiosity. Though the Forest seemed gloriously empty there were a good many hikers on the green tracks and a few genuine tramps drawing unemployment pay from a post office, saving on rent and living life as — in good weather — it should be lived. I could pass as either.

Business for the day was to find a secluded spot not too far from Broom Lodge which I could make my headquarters. I thought the right choice would be one of the conifer woods close-planted by the Forestry Commission, dark and dismal but without anything to attract travelers on foot, who naturally stuck to the great oaks spreading over their waving green sea. First, I quartered a plantation near Staple Edge. That was no good — neither dell nor free mine, too dense and thus with a risk of fire if I lit one. However, it held an outcrop of rock forming an unmistakable landmark, and there I hid the diving kit, which was a nuisance to carry and could attract attention. Then I struck southeast toward Blakeney and found another dense and trackless stand of conifers not far from Broom Lodge.

It covered the side of a steep hill, pockmarked by the typical depressions which might be due to Romans after iron or free miners after coal. Exploration led me to a level patch where the timber was thin enough to admit some sunlight. A building, which may have been a large cottage or a small iron foundry, had stood there once and its site had not been completely cleared by the foresters. The bricks of an outside lavatory still stood to a height of some four feet — a waterproof den if I could find a roof for the three sides. That was provided by a rusty base plate from some engine. When a lever and a ramp of loose stones had got it into position I covered it with dead branches so that it looked like a rubbish heap to be burned when the woods were safely wet. More twigs laid over the turf beneath formed a bed — uncomfortable but still a bed. As for fire, there was no danger whatever, for among the ruins was the blackened dome of a hearth with a few courses of chimney. Industrial rather than sylvan peace, but it served very well. There was no sign that gypsies or enterprising small boys had ever pushed through to the heart of the plantation — no paper bags, plastic bottles or travelers' turds.

All morning while eyes and legs were searching for a home, mind had been pondering the major's question: did Marrin make the golden cauldron or was it ancient work? That rich, two-handled vessel, primitive but exquisitely curved, might be Saxon or a Roman import from the East. I am no authority on art and without an original in front of me for comparison I could not tell. In any case this conjecture came up against a dead end. Why the smoke screen of alchemy and the yarn of a win on the football pools if

Marrin had discovered and dug up an ancient hoard from tomb or temple when he could have made a fortune even after splitting with the state or the landowner?

I could not give the answer, but I was convinced that I was on the right track. Whatever he had found — and the Forest with its ancient mines and ports was as likely a place as any to unearth a buried treasure — he was keeping quiet about it and iniquitously melting it down himself to support his bloody colony of cranks.

I was at last very content that the major had advised me to remain dead. I was free to study Marrin's movements without his ever dreaming that in his mysterious excursions a silent follower was closely behind ready to expose him and rescue for posterity what treasure was left. Now that I had a home, I could familiarize myself with my territory as cautiously as any animal. I was about to write hunted animal, but that was false. I was an animal with a grudge and my quarry was human.

Never before had I realized how unforgiving is the conflict between the sacredness of knowledge and the acquisitiveness of the greedy, whether for the sake of personal wealth or the propagation of a creed, positive right against a wretched negative. Marrin would put it the other way around, convinced to the extent of murder.

In spite of the major's sound advice I might well have decided against meeting him that evening if he had not uttered the words "with the rations." Since Elsa's sandwiches the night before I had had nothing to eat except a slab of greasy fried fish bought from a passing van. Shops anywhere near my headquarters were to be avoided. The corpse was learning that continual caution was needed if it was to stay dead among the living.

The map showed me that Little Drybrook was a hamlet safely far from Broom Lodge which could be reached by forest tracks. I arrived early to reconnoiter the surroundings and waited just off the roadside. His battered car was unmistakable.

"Ah! Glad to see you. Fixed up? Better be! Rain tonight," he said as soon as I stopped the car.

"I can keep it out."

"Used to open air life? Not all books?"

"Not all books. Camels, donkeys, canoes — you name it. I've traveled by it."

"Middle East?"

"Middle East."

"Colder up here."

"Colder in Greeenland."

"Been there too?"

His voice sounded regretful when, finding myself slipping into his staccato speech, I spoke of the extreme climates I had known. Since he had been just too young for the war he may have seen little active service. Possibly the unexciting existence of a regular soldier had unhinged a too contemplative mind and inclined him toward dreams of a past in which war for the sake of Christianity was the normal spice of life. He'd have done better to choose the Crusades, but I suppose the very dubious Arthur gave more scope for imagination.

"Good man! Thought you'd manage! But you'll need a blanket."

He handed over a splendid carriage rug dating from the time when there were no car heaters and told me to take it with me when I left.

"Jump in! Short run into the Forest where we won't be interrupted."

He had found an idyllic spot between the armchair roots of a noble oak where he opened his picnic basket. It had a luxurious air of the eighteen nineties about it and had belonged, he told me, to his grandfather. Gin, whisky, white Burgundy, strawberries and half a cold Severn salmon appeared, each from its proper compartment.

"Couldn't swipe anything from Broom Lodge," he said, "so I got it in Lydney and hung about till the chap had cooked it for me. Ought to know how. Catches them."

While we were eating I encouraged him to talk of his religion. He was as sure of immortality as any pious Christian but considered that Marrin's belief in reincarnation was an unnecessary theory. I ventured to bring up the question of Arthur's battles in which he himself seemed to be personally involved; then he only choked on his salmon and raised an emotional, hot-gospeler's voice to declare that the past was always the present.

"What's the past? Only a string of presents one after another. No such thing as time, Simeon says. He's quite right there. So the past is always the present if you can recognize it. That's the difficulty: to recognize the fourth dimension when you're in it. Could draw a diagram if I were a mathematician."

Having cordially accepted the string-of-presents theory as expounded by Major Quixote — there's a flaw in it somewhere, but it does account for visions of the past — I started on the strawberries and asked him how much he knew of Marrin's movements.

"Too busy to leave the place in the day much unless he's off to London to sell his trinkets, but he does go out at night when the tide serves his purpose. Meditating underwater they say."

"And if I want to leave a message for you, how shall I do it?"

He asked if I was sure that I could find again the ragged stump of the sapling he had cut. Yes, I was sure.

"Then bury your note alongside and put in a stick to mark it. I'll do the same."

It was now twilight. I thanked him warmly and got up to go.

"Any trouble with alcohol?" he asked.

"No trouble."

"Good! Take the whisky bottle."

I thanked him warmly again and left, but did not go home. First I watched the major drive away; he was shaking his head and talking to himself when he got into the car, perhaps in sadness at the criminality of his enigmatic friend. Then I set out on foot for Broom Lodge. I reckoned that if there was anything at all in this meditation over the flowing tide Marrin, after last night, would have a good deal to meditate about and might get down to it straightaway.

It was nearly dark when I arrived so that I was perfectly safe in the garden on the open front of the house. Lights were on in the hall for those who preferred earnest discussion to bed; lights were going off upstairs as craftsmen and farmhands who would be up early settled down to sleep. It occurred to me that if Simeon Marrin wished to give his disappearances an air of spiritual mystery he would slip away at the back into the shadow of the trees rather than walk out the front door like ordinary humanity; so I made a circuit into the woodland at the back and waited.

A little before midnight eight persons left the house and took the forest track into the darkness. I could tell by his height that one of them was Marrin who carried a box. Another appeared to be carrying a trumpet. When they had passed, I followed. I had no experience of this sort of prowling, but it seemed simple enough so long as the pursued made enough noise, however slight, to cover the sound of the pursuer. Of that there was little, for I kept to the soft grass in the middle of the ride and was ultracareful where I stepped.

It was soon plain that their destination was not the river but somewhere deep in the Forest. They stopped at last in an open space between the oaks where the young green bracken was thick over the brown mat of last year's fronds. Marrin used a powerful flashlight to satisfy himself that there was no one in the immediate neighborhood but omitted to search beyond tree trunks. It looked as if an open-air ceremony was about to begin. That did not surprise me. I had thought all along that the commune was very secular — plenty of casual discussions and meetings but, apart from the hours of meditation, no set ritual. I had expected from that druidical inner circle robes, invocations and other impressive mumbo jumbo.

Now I got it, and in that setting indeed impressive. The trumpet was not a trumpet but the torch of old time. When stuck in the ground and lit, it threw a steady, smoky red light over the proceedings, allowing me to see that Marrin was clothed in a long blue robe. He opened the casket I had seen in the laboratory and took out the golden cauldron, lifting it high above his head by the two handles with the gesture of a priest. Its weight was obvious, and I was again convinced by its triumphant simplicity that it was ancient. While one of his seven tonsured acolytes chanted in a low voice some language that I think was old Welsh — as near as one could get to the vernacular in which British seamen and miners would have prayed to Nodens if they had no Latin — Marrin passed the cauldron to another. A third, who carried a covered pot, lifted the lid and poured the contents into the cauldron. A strong, intoxicating scent of herbs and honey came downwind to me. Meanwhile the remaining four stamped out a circle in the bracken with Marrin in the center. When it was complete, one of them passed the cauldron back to Marrin across the circumference.

The object of the rite so far as I could guess — and since the language of gestures is universal one tends to guess right — was to propitiate or help the spirits of the dead. I don't wonder that Marrin had called a conclave of adepts. I'm going to need quite a lot of propitiation. He did not mention my name. To him alone the ceremony had special meaning.

The seven adepts appeared to see and to bless some sort of apparition in the air above the bowl. The curious thing is that I saw it myself: a diaphanous, moving figure like a pencil of mist rising from the ground. My brain of course was affected by the brew in the bowl and mistranslating the message from the eyes. I have no doubt that Marrin saw it too. He was not playacting this time. He believed so absolutely in himself and his rite that he created the illusion for the rest of us, perhaps by telepathy and the hypnotic effect of the drug. Proof that it was illusion? First, that I wasn't dead at all and only he thought I was. Second, that all the codswallop of solemnities could produce the desired effect on a profane, skeptical outsider, unclean ritually and in fact.

They spent about half an hour on the In Memoriam service and returned to Broom Lodge as secretly as they had set out. I followed in order to see what door they used in case it ever came in handy and then walked home to my den — feeling myself a ghost wandering among trees and tracks, for on the way I did not pass man or sheep, partly due to the late hour and a slight drizzle which had started.

Tucked up in my outside lavatory with the major's rug over me and a good swig of his whisky inside me I thought over the curious scene. Was such liturgy at the heart of Broom Lodge? I thought not. It was confined to the druidical dropouts — a vulgar nickname of mine considering the woodland features of the ceremony handed down from pagan and poetical Britons. I knew the names of four of them: the chanter, Evans, a sulky fellow who strutted like a hierarch, which Marrin never did; Raeburn, who poured the brew into the cauldron, an excellent craftsman with a sense of humor in daily life; Ballard, the curate-looking chap who had been digging up tulips when I first arrived; and Carver, a compact, little holy man who passed the cauldron to Marrin.

Evidently it was such a rite as this which the major suspected and considered a blasphemous misuse of the cauldron, far worse than the half-pagan heresies somehow related to the mysteries of metals. Transmutation I did not believe, but those herbs of which the heavy scent flowed off under the branches farther than the smoke of the torch suggested that Marrin was a devoted student of ancestral pharmacy and that the laboratory itself was no pretense.

I slept long and late, recovering from the two nights and such exercise as I had not taken since tracing the once cultivated fields on the coast of Greenland. I found myself stiff but fit. The first job was to buy supplies from somewhere miles away where I had never been before. Coleford to the north and on the edge of the Forest seemed a likely spot. It turned out to be an ugly little Victorian town like most of the mining settlements, but with everything I needed. Having noticed a fire-watching tower which commanded most of the Forest I decided against using my ruined hearth in case the plume of smoke was noticed, and bought a Primus stove and a frying pan. With eggs, butter, cheese, bread fresh from the oven, meat, green stuff and a variety of cans plus a bottle of brandy to disguise the taste of coal in the sparkling water from the nearest stream I returned home to my plantation.

My mind was blank on how and where to make my next attack on Broom Lodge. According to the major, Marrin seldom left the estate during the day. Night — well, it was pointless to go out every night in the hope of something happening. The best bet was for the corpse to create some diversion in order to walk off with that chalice and obtain an expert's opinion.

In the reddish light of the torch the two-handled cauldron had again looked to me of great age. Could it be, I wondered, that Marrin was passing off his own work as two thousand years old or better? Highly improbable that he could deceive the authorities at the British Museum! And if he had, we should all have heard of the extraordinary find. The papers would be full of it.

A photograph then from several angles. The major could probably manage that. But would photographs of the cauldron be enough to tell an expert whether the goldsmith was living or long dead? I doubted it. However, once my mind began to run on photographs a secondary object presented itself. How about some shots of the turtle? I knew a zoologist who would remember me well though I had not seen him for some years. He could give me his opinion by return mail if I asked for it. The beast could not be so obscure that neither he nor his colleagues could fail to identify it.

At any rate it was a scheme to fill up an otherwise empty day. So I wrote a note to the major:

*Can you secretly take some close-up photographs of the turtle in his laboratory and leave them here? I believe they may give us a line on what he is doing.*

This time I was very careful in approaching Broom Lodge from the back, avoiding the paths, moving from tree to tree and ready to drop into the bracken at any moment. I had more trouble than I expected in finding the stump of the ash sapling. That done, I covered the letter with a cushion of moss and marked it with a white sliver of wood.

No one was about except a party of two men and two girls on the nearest track, walking in a dream of the Forest of Arden and prettily singing a madrigal, so I determined to have a look in daylight at the open space where my wandering spirit had received attention. That, too, took some finding, for there were many places where the oaks stood far enough apart to form a glade, though none had the beaten-down bracken between them. I doubt if I ever would have found it if not for the glimpse of another person moving across my front. I turned on to a parallel course and arrived at the outer pillars of the woodland sanctuary, on the opposite side to my position the night before.

I recognized him. He was Carver, whom I had often seen packing a primitive kiln with bricks to be fired — hard physical labor which he carried out with a set contented smile. Those smiles were one of the most exasperating features of the tonsured, expressing a false puritanical humility of the saved. During the ceremony he appeared to have lost something, for he was now searching through and under the squashed bracken, moving methodically over the ground he had covered the previous night.

After some twenty minutes he gave up and started back. I was curious to know what he had dropped and, as so often happens when a fresh pair of eyes takes over a search, found the missing article near the circumference of the circle. It was his wristwatch and hard to see since it was face downward with the back encased in dark-green leather. The strap was worn and half split, and the watch must have fallen from his wrist when he stretched out across the beaten circle to pass the bowl to Marrin. Obviously neither of them had noticed it, being entranced by fumes and piety.

I picked it up and would have liked to return it. After all, it had been lost in an act of kindly monkeying with my soul. But even returning it through the major would lead to far too many questions. So I decided to leave it where Carver or one of his fellows could not miss it — not difficult since I knew the path by which they went out and back. Some of the colony's pigs were rooting and grubbing not far away, covering any noise I made and allowing me to walk normally. He at the same time must have been dreaming of enlightenment or in no hurry to return to heaving bricks, for I found that I had got ahead of him. I laid the watch in the middle of the track face upward with a shaft of sunlight falling directly on it through the leaves, and slipped back into the bracken to see what he would do.

He didn't miss it. He couldn't. He picked it up with an exclamation of astonishment, raised his hands, murmured something I couldn't hear and looked upward into all the branches around as if assuming that some bird had dropped the watch into his path. Then he continued to Broom Lodge almost at a run. His manner was so peculiar and excited that I was bursting with curiosity and followed, slipping into the tall, pink foxgloves from which, the day before, I had watched the back of the house and caught a glimpse of Elsa.

Now it was that I perceived a new facet of that many-sided man, Simeon Marrin. He was fraud, idealist and a born leader — like so many of them not excluding murder when needful — but I had not suspected him of being superstitious. Perhaps superstitious is the wrong word. It implies illogicality, whereas the ritual I had witnessed showed that he had worked out or accepted some sort of purgatory as a consequence of the transition from one life to another. Carver dashed into the estate office and almost immediately came out with Marrin. He was showing him the watch, miraculously transported to the spot where he could not miss it, but the other, so far as I could see, was not overimpressed until Carver pointed to the broken strap. Then Marrin's face quite evidently displayed a sudden gravity, even shock. The broken strap had no special meaning for Carver, but for Marrin it was an instant reminder of the cunning weakening of the straps on the open heel fins. My spirit by a neat piece of telekinesis — I was always good with my hands — had established its identity. Inspired guesswork, but I am sure I am right.

I left for the rock where I had deposited the diving kit and waited there until it was dark and I could walk home with the Aqualung without attracting attention. I had no immediate use for it, but I could foresee that Severn and Forest were equally likely to hold the clue to the hoard which Marrin was ransacking. I think it was that night when my attitude toward him changed. After a solid, much-needed supper I lay on my bed of twigs, concentrating not so much on the mystery of the gold but on my quarry. In my mind I called him that because I hoped to track him through the Forest as relentlessly as a carnivore. If the druidicals knew how my thoughts were running and believed in such things — was there any damned nonsense they weren't ready to believe? — they could call me possessed, though in fact I wanted Marrin alive, well and talking. At any rate I slept as soundly as any satisfied werewolf.

Off again in the morning to find a message from the major at the foot of the sapling:

> *Easy. He left me alone there. Perhaps we are assuming guilt where there isn't any. Mining. Naturally keeps it quiet. Are you sure your misfortune was not accident? Meet me tomorrow same place eleven a.m.*

My misfortune, hell! But of course he wanted to believe in his hero if it was at all possible. In spite of that our interests were the same. He had put it plainly enough when he said that he must keep Marrin out of jail. As for me I was determined to prevent a crime more monstrous than murder. I was a little suspicious of that phrase "left me alone there." But after all why shouldn't the major be left alone there? He was a welcome guest and an old friend and it did not matter if he wandered around investigating chemicals. It was proof of his value to me as an ally, so long as he could keep his mouth shut and did not go chasing after preposterous ideas like mining. There might be some stream in the Forest where you could pick up a few grains by panning, but you could not dig a hole as in the Klondike and find sizable nuggets at the bottom.

I did not approve of another roadside meeting in daylight. The major was taking this business of staying dead as casually as a game of hide-and-seek. However, he discreetly parked his car among the trees, waiting patiently until I appeared and signaled to him to join me. He showed me three excellent pictures of the turtle, well lit from the opposite window of the laboratory, showing a side view of head and tail and a front view of the head. I noticed for the first time that there was no skeleton, only the curious armadillo-like carapace covering the whole animal.

"What did Simeon tell you about it?" he asked.

"That he had put it up for fun."

"Just like him! See you don't believe it! Think he bought it?"

"Possibly. But if he just wanted to impress his public a skeleton of a crocodile would have done — and cheaper."

Marrin at the time had been holding forth — quite sincerely — on the life of the tideway from lamprey to salmon so that I felt the remains of the turtle were probably from one of the Severn deeps, either discovered by him in the silt or perhaps on the mantelpiece of the lonely cottage of some salmon fisher. I asked the major to run into nearby Bream and come back with a sheet of paper and a stamped envelope. When he returned I sent the photographs to my colleague in the zoology department and asked him to let me know urgently what the creature was, addressing his reply to me at the Bream Post Office as I was continually on the move.

"I've been thinking," the major said. "Simeon could have dug it up down a mine."

"What is this about mining?"

"Keeps a pick and spade and a drum of nylon cord in the trunk of his car. What for?"

"To bury my body if it turns up."

"Might be anywhere, old boy. Police bound to find it first."

"Free bucket of coal? Digging up daffodil bulbs?"

"Goes off for the day sometimes with Evans and Carver. We ought to follow the car."

"You can follow if you like. I'm not risking it," I said firmly.

"What about a false beard or something?"

Typical of him! I had only the clothes I stood up in and my voice was easily recognizable. It was a perfect formula for disaster.

"Do you know where they go?"

"Wigpool Common. A company mined for gold there years ago."

"Try your luck alone then but don't get caught snooping!"

I reminded him that Marrin was determined to keep his secrets and that friendship would not count at all in an emergency.

"Locals say there is an underground lake. Bloody rabbit warren, they say. Full of tunnels. Iron. Romans. Why would they want an underground lake anyway?"

"Communing with spirits of the earth."

"Ah yes! Hadn't thought of that. Very reasonable."

"But gold more reasonable still, you think?"

"Might be both."

"Snow White and the Seven Dwarfs?"

"You mustn't laugh at legends, Piers. There's always some truth in them if you can spot where it is. Next time I'm going to watch 'em."

I told him to be very careful that afterward he wasn't watched himself, and I insisted he should not try to meet me until I told him when and where. Meanwhile all communications should be by the stump of the sapling, and I would call there every morning.

No doubt the major was on to something of interest, relevant or not. I would have liked to know what was the significance of Wigpool Common, but this new eccentricity of Marrin and his inner circle confirmed how helpless I was. I could watch the comings and goings at Broom Lodge; I could explore the banks of the Severn; but I could not follow Marrin if he left by car and most certainly not in company with the major, whose distinctive Humber was sure to be spotted. If asked by Marrin what the devil he thought he was doing, his only hope was to stutter one of his staccato replies which could mean anything.

So, when the major had driven away, there was nothing for it but to walk home to my comfortable ex-lavatory, stopping on the way to buy a daily paper and any other reading matter that Bream might have and, if there was an off-license, supplies of something better than my coal-tasting stream.

Bream was far enough from Broom Lodge to make it unlikely that any members of the commune would be about. Their normal shopping town was Lydney. After sliding, not too obviously, from cover to cover like a soldier afraid of snipers, I completed my purchases, passed the butcher's, saw some mutton kidneys in the window and thought how good they would be grilled on a wooden spit. When I had paid for them and was just going out Elsa appeared from the living quarters behind the shop.

"Piers!"

"And you — what are you doing here?"

"Selling black puddings. I thought you were in Wales."

"Are you alone? Did anyone drive you over?"

"I bicycled. I'm trying to get a contract from dear Mr. Willets."

"And she's got it," said Mr. Willets, impressed by the "dear" in such a lovely mouth.

"At forty pence a pound?"

"Don't leave me much profit, Miss Marrin, but it's a deal."

We walked out together, myself torn between the delight of seeing her and anxiety lest this might be the end of my staying dead.

"You haven't shaved and you smell of coal and dried leaves," she said.

"Only my clothes. It's just that I slept rough last night. I couldn't find a room anywhere so I played Robin Hood in the greenwood."

"Come back with me and clean up!"

That gave me an opportunity.

"Think how hurt they would be if I just came back to have a bath and cleared off!"

"Then come back and stay with us again! You'd be welcome. Simeon liked you."

I said that I knew that and had liked him. It wasn't a lie. I had.

"But you know how difficult it was for us," I reminded her.

"I don't care if we do shock them."

"But much better if we can meet and you don't say a word. When can I see you?"

"Whenever you like, if you *do* like."

"Tomorrow afternoon in your dell?"

"If I can."

She pedaled off. I was fairly confident that she would not speak of our meeting, not for the reason I had given but because she knew instinctively that I had a better reason and had not told her all the truth.

For the rest of the day there was nothing for it but to be patient and wish to God that she was not the fond niece of Simeon Marrin. Next morning I went over to the woods behind Broom Lodge to see if the major had left any message for me. I was now familiar with the shortest route by tracks and footpaths through the Forest and often passed the time of day with other walkers. That was unimportant since no one knew who I was. The risk of meeting any of the colonists was very slight. They were dutifully busy at their tasks with neither time nor inclination for casual strolls.

I found a report from the major militarily precise and piously long, which I had to read more than twice before it was clear that even for him mining was ruled out. He had gone to Wigpool Common on foot in the afternoon and apparently behaved as sensibly as any private investigator. Tea at a teashop. One pub at eighteen hours. Another at eighteen-thirty. I think soldiers must be trained to leave out all illuminating details in their reports. Yes, the place was riddled with underground shafts but the entrances were all blocked up. Iron mining it had been, not coal. Yes, there was supposed to be a large cavern with a pool in it. Strangers had been casually poking about after gold for years, encouraged by rumors rather than geology. A tall man with one or two companions often drove out and was digging near the Bailey Rock. Not for gold. They were in the wrong place for that. They didn't say much, and were accepted as geologists.

I gathered that the local inhabitants took such visitors as all in the day's work. Whether scientists or romanticists, they caused no excitement in a village of former miners for whom the pattern of galleries under their feet was as familiar as the pattern of galaxies to an astronomer. Marrin of course might have come across a hoard in some solitary dig, but that he could keep it secret was most unlikely. All the evidence I had still pointed to the bank of the Severn.

The lake or pool might certainly exist in old iron workings since even the modern coal mines had been closed down because of the expense of pumping. Whether the pool was or was not in a natural cavern seemed doubtful. The only essential question for us was why Marrin and his assistants did not talk about their excavations — probably for the same reason that they did not talk about their forest ceremonies. I might not be far out in my wild guess that they were introducing themselves to long-suffering spirits of lower earth.

In the early afternoon I set out for Elsa's private dell and had trouble in finding it since I had been paying attention to her rather than the path she took. So I returned quickly to the track by which we had left Broom Lodge, waited for her and then followed her. It was not safe to show myself so near the colony and walk alongside her.

She was nervous and not very happy, once or twice stopping as if to return. That was understandable. I may have appeared to her a mere seducer anxious to keep our affair quiet and in no hurry to see her again. She had nothing to go on, knew not enough about me and was calling herself a sucker.

I had shaved, but otherwise looked what I was: a tramp in the Forest. The darling took command from the start, kissing me like a sister with arms on my shoulders.

"Piers, you needn't be so proud," she said. "Why didn't you tell me you had no money?"

It was, after all, an intelligent guess that I couldn't afford an inn and I wouldn't sponge on the colony. I was half tempted to let her explanation stand, for it would save a lot of trouble. On the other hand, she might quite easily ignore my demand for secrecy and tell Uncle that he was to insist on putting me up even if I refused.

What I did was to give her some account of my travels which I had barely mentioned since the first dinner at Broom Lodge. When one is studying communities of the past, I said, one must live as they did to understand their economies. That was of course non-sense, but it sounded impressive and she cheered up.

"Your Romans had hot baths, Piers," she retorted.

"But the tribes of the Forest didn't."

"Why don't you try plowing a field with a flint on the end of a digging stick?"

"Unnecessary. I'd be more interested in the mining and trading of the flints."

She accused me of being an absentminded professor, and I asked her if she thought they couldn't fall in love.

"And then hide just around the corner for three days when they are supposed to be in Wales and don't write or telephone!"

"Of course I hid. I didn't want you to find me smelling of old coal."

"I said leaves."

"You don't mind that?"

She did not answer, but stood there, tall and serene, with her eyes on a level with mine, and no longer questioning, but surrendering.

When at last we drew apart from each other and lay side by side on our backs looking up into the approving, quivering canopy of leaves, my conscience pricked. I longed for the peace and passion of her to continue; they had and they would, but I felt like some spy who had learned to love with all his heart, disgusted that he must interrogate the girl who trusted him, yet determined to do so.

"Does Simeon still try to spear salmon?" I asked.

"Not since the win on the pools. But he still goes out at night."

"Spirits of the deep?"

"Something of the sort! I don't understand that silly lot who treat him as an archdruid. He shouldn't put up with an inner circle like that in our colony. I wish he'd stick to meditation and past lives and all that."

"Perhaps he believes he's an archdruid?" I suggested.

"Well, he can if he likes so long as he doesn't try it on you and me and the rest of them."

She knew very little of the sect and its activities. At twenty-two there is so much one doesn't notice — or can't be bothered to notice — outside the play of characters and the daily complications of a job. If she had been told that her uncle chose to stand on his head and let gold grow out of his feet, she would have shrugged her shoulders, wondered what he was really up to and got on with mothering the colony and selling black puddings.

"Do they ever go skin diving with him?"

"I'm sure they don't. He likes to be alone. I was surprised when he took you down to the Guscar Rocks."

"So was I. He wanted to show me that it was not dangerous at slack water. But there can't be many places where one can go in off the land."

"He has a boat — a little dinghy with an outboard motor."

"At Lydney?"

"No. Higher up at Bullo Pill."

It was mere chance that she knew where it was. The boat came from a barge which was being broken up. Marrin had paid cash for it and the transaction should never have appeared in the books at all; but the buyer's receipt had accidentally passed through her hands, stating the price of the dinghy plus delivery at Bullo. She didn't know if it was still there.

"That was before he took to his goldsmith's work?" I asked.

"About the same time."

The scanty evidence suggested that he had bought the boat after he had found the hoard and because it was easier or safer to transport the precious objects by water rather than by land. In that case where was it? The grave or treasury could not be underwater since the level of the Severn would not have changed much in the last fifteen hundred years, though its course certainly had. So it must be in some place where there had been dry land at the time, say, of the worship of Nodens and was underwater now. Yet there were few if any such places. Everywhere the floodplain of the tideway had been wider than now.

Well then, Marrin might have discovered the hoard in or on the banks. Very unlikely. No one would bury a chieftain and his treasure where an exceptional tide might sweep the lot away. I came to the conclusion that boat and hoard had nothing to do with each other. Marrin continued to use the boat because he was fascinated, spiritually and physically, by life beneath the waters.

My darling abbess more easily accepted my explanation of leading an Iron Age life. The fact was, I think, that she found our woodland lovemaking so precious and romantic that not even Uncle was to be informed of my secret presence. We agreed to meet again and after that I would soon reappear at Broom Lodge as a respectable townsman. The distressing thought occurred to me that, if I did, Simeon Marrin's fate would be in my hands. Attempted murder need not for Elsa's sake be followed up, but the monstrous destruction of a treasure — or, as the major feared, the production of fakes — would have to be exposed.

The next task after leaving Elsa was to explore Bullo Pill, which I had never seen. It was some four miles away and if I went there at once I should avoid the long tramp back to my den and out again. I expected an ugly jumble of decaying dumps and buildings, for I knew that it had once been a little port where barges loaded coal for transport across the river to Arlingham.

Reality was very different. When I passed under the railway bridge from farmland to the usual close-cropped meadow of the Severn banks there was hardly a sign of industry but the two stone buttresses at the entrance to the pill, which was a valley of mud some thirty feet deep and as much across with the usual insignificant stream at the bottom. On the northern bank were a group of three cottages and a small factory behind them.

The southern bank reminded me of an archaeological site where the turf has been replaced and only the lines of foundations can be detected. This Severnside lawn ran away for quarter of a mile in even beauty bounded inland by a delicious avenue of great hawthorns, perhaps the remains of a double hedge. Along the river front were stone bollards to which barges must have tied up while waiting for the tide. There could never have been room for more than three or four inside the pill.

At the end of the lawn was another pill, a narrow gorge twelve feet deep, running along the side of a copse. Suddenly I realized that this was where I had been hurled ashore. Since I had crawled out of the slime into this thicket and gone straight for the Forest I had never seen Bullo Pill and its cottages.

Marrin indeed had found privacy here. It seemed to be a better spot for personal meditation than Broom Lodge, here where the clock of one's life would be governed only by the ebb and flow of the Severn, which ran smoothly down this reach at its game of pretending to be one of the great navigable highways from Europe to ocean. There could be no doubt which was Marrin's boat: a ten-foot dinghy with an outboard lying in the pill along with a salmon boat and a decaying motor cruiser, all laid up on a terrace of mud waiting for the tide to lift them. The dinghy was too small to be used for diving and confirmed my growing opinion that he always went in off the land.

A woman came out of one of the cottages and crossed the head of the pill. After some conversation in which I congratulated her on living in so lovely a spot — she was well aware of it, bless her, with no complaints of isolation! — I asked her if the dinghy was hers. No, she said, it belonged to a gentleman from up the Forest who used it just for crossing the river. She giggled that she supposed he had a friend in Arlingham and slipped over to see her without going all the way around by Gloucester.

That was easy enough. Marrin could reach his dinghy at half tide and go down on the ebb when the channel would sweep him away to the opposite bank. There he would have to wait for the flood before returning to Bullo Pill — a matter of anything up to eight hours. What did he do meanwhile? Whatever it was — digging or diving or merely collecting — took place on the other side of the Severn.

There was another useful inference to be drawn. If he wanted to be back at Broom Lodge at or before dawn he would have to choose a night when five or six hours were left in the ebb, wait till the bore had passed and grab the short, favorable tide flowing up behind it.

After a night of dozing rather than sleeping I woke up impatient for action, the more so as there seemed no chance of any at all. The business of staying dead was boring me and my determination to destroy Marrin one way or another was weakened by the thought of its effect on Elsa. After taking the walk out to the sapling and back in case the major had left a message — sure that if he had it would be crazily impractical — I spent the day like a frustrated housewife, adding twigs to my bed and tying them down, stopping a drip from the iron roof and eating two large meals to make up for a great deal of exercise on an empty stomach. A party of campers walked around two sides of my copse but never attempted to enter it, confirming my opinion that it was a safe refuge. But a refuge for what?

Next day at least one mystery was solved, though of little importance. For want of anything better to do I called at the Bream Post Office. It was unlikely that I could already have a reply from the department of zoology, but the letter was waiting for me. Evidently the beast was so well known that my colleague had not needed to refer to library or museum.

Your photographs are of a magnificent specimen of glyptodont. Though the solid shell over the back does resemble that of a turtle, the plates over head and tail are segmented. Bones have rotted away, as one would expect, but carapace and armor are largely intact, preserved, I think, by being buried in silt. Microscope will show. When can I see it? Glyptodont is not a reptile but an extinct mammal related to the armadillo and — to judge by the skull — comparatively intelligent. Yours was a young animal, a half-grown glyptodont kitten shall we say? The spiked tail may have been used for smashing into termite nests or as a mace for walloping predators while they tried to get their teeth into the armor. So far as we know, the animal existed only in America and may well have been contemporary with man like the extinct giant sloth. Where was it found? Come back quickly and tell us. If in this country, the discovery is unique.

Silt. Another clue to the Severn. When I asked Marrin about the supposed turtle he gave me the unsatisfactory answer that he had set up the remains in his laboratory for fun. He never said that he himself had found it underwater or dug it up. Why not? Probable explanation: because it came from a site he wished to keep secret.

So off again to the stump of the sapling. The major was there waiting for me, and I was not too pleased to see him, preferring written messages which gave me time to think — very necessary when dealing with a wandering friar, as he had called himself, who was a preposterous visionary inside and shrewd outside, so that it was doubtful if even he knew what was going on at the interface where they met.

He had been waiting a couple of hours. His mustache had perked up and his watery blue eyes had dried to a sparkle.

"Got an idea, Piers!" he exclaimed. "Brilliant! But tell me if you don't think so. Remember how Simeon left me alone to take those photographs? All stems from that. Shocking breach of trust, but for his own good. And he needn't know. Make it plain it was burglary."

Since my mind was running on glyptodonts and tides, I translated these enthusiastic explosions as referring to Marrin's diving kit or the tools in the back of his van. The object of burglary turned out to be the golden cauldron. The major was proposing to steal it and hand it to me for submission to some authority who could tell us whether it was ancient work or not and, if it wasn't, whether it had any chance of being sold as such.

"He'll be out fishing tonight," the major said. "So we have to hurry. Last-minute plan. Often effective. Catches 'em on the wrong foot."

"How do you know he'll be out?"

"Simple. Been watching him. Saw him loading the gear into his van."

"But he's careful not to be observed."

"All them at work except me. After dark I'll burst in and grab the bowl for you. Then you take the first train up to London and you could be back with it in the afternoon."

It was very likely that he would be out either on that night or the next. The tide fitted the crossing from Bullo in the late evening and the return before dawn.

However, I doubted my ability to charge into the British Museum, dressed as I was, with a valuable object of gold and avoid immediate arrest. It depended on whether I could get an introduction and a guarantee of good faith in the short time available. I doubted still more if the major could commit a fake burglary without being caught.

"Nothing to it if I don't slip up somewhere," he said. "And if I do, I've got a dozen stories to explain what I was up to."

His scheme as he presented it seemed as if it had been conceived under the Round Table with an intoxicated Arthur; but the more he spluttered, the more I saw that it was quite likely to work. Burglars, I was sure, had never been seriously considered by the commune. Outsiders knew nothing of Marrin's products. There were no other valuables, and no burglar would risk breaking in when people were awake and about at all hours.

The lab was at the back of the east wing. Windows were set high up so that no passersby could see in, and the window at the north end facing the Forest was not overlooked by any of the bedrooms. Access was from the estate office by a door which was locked. The key, the major assured me, was kept in a drawer of Marrin's desk — on the face of it a casual and too confident arrangement, but the hold Marrin had over his colonists must be remembered. None of them would have entered the holy of holies unless invited.

I asked the major how he was going to make such a simple job look like a burglary from outside.

"Easy! Chap got in by climbing the drainpipe. Pipe passes within a couple of feet of the north window."

"But can you climb it?"

"Of course I can. Always was good at P.T. But I'm not going to. I'm going down it."

His plan was feasible. Having entered the lab from the estate office he would open the north window and quietly smash the pane nearest to the catch (he knew about brown paper and molasses) so that the glass fell into the room. Then he proposed to mess up the room in true burglar fashion and break into the casket where the bowl was kept, grab it, and leave by the drainpipe so that police or colonists could readily spot the marks of the burglar's passage. He reckoned he could just about reach the pipe from the window.

"One snag," I told him. "You are leaving the door from the estate office unlocked."

"No, I'm not. When I'm safely on the ground, I can nip back to the estate office through the front door, lock the lab and shove the key back in the drawer. Great care all around. Wear gloves. Take cover when in doubt. Never hurry."

"Suppose someone pops out of a bedroom when you're passing."

"Don't care if he does. I'm on the way to have a piss. Some of 'em never waste it indoors. Good for the trees. May be right. Very sensible some of their beliefs!"

I told him that he would have to take some gold trinkets as well as the cauldron to make the burglary convincing.

"Yes, bothers me how we're going to put them back," he said.

"We don't put them back or the cauldron till we have a quiet interview with him. He'll talk all right. Just seeing me alive will be enough to break him down."

"Suppose he really did make the bowl?"

"Well, if he did and has been buying gold in the market all along, we'll be left with the problem of how the hell he makes enough profit to keep Broom Lodge running."

For the major's sake I hoped the burglary would succeed, but what excited me far more was that Marrin had loaded his diving kit into his van. I no longer had to keep an eye indefinitely at Bullo for him to appear and then — if my patience lasted — to watch all night for his return.

I pointed out to the major that I could not take the cauldron up to London straightaway and that he would have to hide it for at least twenty-four hours while I rested — if that was necessary — and arranged the next move. I asked him to drive to Gloucester at once and to buy me a pair of fins at the best sports shop. Then he was to meet me at our usual place outside Drybrook about quarter past nine and take me to Bullo where Marrin kept his boat.

"Didn't know he had one!"

"Well, he does. And wherever he goes he'll have to wait for the turn of the tide to get back to Bullo; so you'll have all night for the burglary and can take your time."

All went according to plan. When he met me at Drybrook I curled up on the floor of the car, inconspicuous under the rug and the life jacket, and slid out at the little lane to Bullo. Denzil was to drive on upriver and then make a detour to Broom Lodge so that there would be no chance of Marrin's passing him on the road and recognizing his car.

It was a warm, still evening, overcast, with not a sound but the lapping of the ebb against the stonework at the entrance to the pill. I lay down at the beginning of the avenue of hawthorn where I could watch all movement on the banks. Marrin turned up about ten in the last of the light, on foot and carrying all his diving kit in a case made to fit rather than my own untidy bundle. When he had gone down out of sight, I trotted along the avenue to the bank of the baby pill so that I could keep him in sight as long as possible. He was bound to set off downstream, for no little outboard motor could make way against the speed of the ebb.

All this while I had assumed that he meant to land at Arlingham and then walk along the bank until he arrived at his destination. I could not follow him but I could intercept him on his return. But what good would that do unless he was actually carrying a gold bracelet or some other object from the hoard? I might not be able to bluff him into confessing where he had found it and I should lose all the advantage of being dead.

It was then that I had the wild idea of following him. I could come to no great harm so long as I stayed on or near the surface. I could never catch up with him but I should not be far behind; and wherever he landed or anchored I should be able to make out the empty dinghy. Any success depended on his destination. The tide would carry him down the channel on the left bank for some three miles and then, swinging around the great bank of the Noose would take him back again for about the same distance to the right bank opposite Blakeney. I hardly dared to follow him as far as that though the twirlings and sucklings of the yellow ebb, but on second thought I decided it would not be necessary. If his destination was on the right bank he had no reason to take a boat from Bullo; he had only to leave his car at any crossing of the railway, walk over the even Severn meadows and dive. Anyway that didn't make sense. There could be no finding treasure under the mud.

It was far more likely that he intended to reach some point on the left bank without being carried around the Noose. Hock Cliff, which I had visited on the first day of my Severn ramblings, at once suggested itself. Unlike the red cliffs of the Severn it was a Lower Lias clay and had been eaten back by the tides leaving a flat terrace of rock at the edge of the shore. It was certainly easy to land there, but what for? However, leaving out the inexplicable diving equipment, Hock Cliff was a very possible site for treasure buried long ago on good, solid dry land well above the highest level of the river but now exposed by erosion. It was a theory which could be proved or disproved immediately.

I put on suit, life jacket, mask and Aqualung and dropped into the mouth of the baby pill, being careful to keep my feet off the bottom. Marrin put-putted out of Bullo and passed close inshore but could not possibly see me in the gathering darkness. I slipped out and followed, swimming well clear of the Box Rock, of which only a small part was showing above water. The dinghy was now far ahead of me but occasionally I caught a glimpse of it when it bounced on the vicious wavelets of the ebb and the wake showed white. The sound of the engine told me that he was bound straight down channel and not bearing a little to port as he would if he intended to land below Arlingham. I was about to give up and make for the Arlingham shore myself when the engine stopped and I thought I heard the splash of his heavy anchor — sound traveled half a mile over the sleeping Severn. So I kept on swimming until I could make out the dinghy anchored below the wood at the top of Hock Cliff. There seemed no reason why he should stop there. He still had his clothes on. I think now that he had arrived earlier than he intended and was waiting for the tide to fall a foot or two farther. There turned out to be a handy little inlet in the rock terrace where the dinghy could safely lie when he left it, but he could not yet be sure of its position because the whole terrace was still awash with the ebb dancing over it fast enough to hole or swamp the dinghy if he made a mistake.

I was in danger of being carried past him but managed to reach the edge of the terrace underwater and clung there by my fingers as if I were a climber on a rock face until I found a cleft which enabled me to relax and lift my head to watch the dinghy and Marrin. The ebb spat its silt at me and I remembered my agony in the quicksand. Then came disgust at the ceremony I had witnessed for the propitiation of my soul. Well, it wasn't propitiated. Far from it! I was suddenly exasperated by all this folly — the silly side of them as Elsa had called it. Marrin, I had told the major, would break down as soon as he knew I was alive. And he'd break down worse still if he had a little additional evidence that I was dead.

Looking back I think that I myself was possessed by a devil which knew exactly what it was about. Blood sacrifice and fireworks are unnecessary when there is an eager human spirit ready to give a temporary home. To break him at any cost was what I wanted, to have him gibbering the truth of the gold and his reason for murder.

The dinghy was nearer in than I thought, riding just off a peninsula of the terrace. Marrin had anchored none too soon. I swam along the angle between rock and mud like a Severn lamprey seeking blood to suck until with two good kicks I could reach the mooring. The mysterious jerk on the rope produced some startled movement on board which then quieted down.

With hands and knees grasping the stem and out of sight I put head and shoulders over the bows dressed exactly as I was when he tried to kill me and remained perfectly still. He was standing in the stern looking for the inlet. When he turned around and saw me, he stared, frozen. Then he tried to fend off this motionless phantom with movements of the arms as if he were swimming or clearing a mist of smoke before the eyes. Not surprisingly the dinghy tipped — if I helped it at all it was accidental — and he went overboard with a coughing yell, crashing his head on the outcrop of rock, just underwater, which had allowed my approach. The ebb caught him and swept him away from the boat, and he was on his way down channel with any carcasses and timber which the Severn had gathered to itself since morning.

I heard no more of him and saw nothing. I should have expected Marrin, considering his intimacy with spirits, at least to try to talk to my uneasy ghost instead of panicking. I hoped he would be swept ashore on the sands of the Noose. God knows I did not want him dead, for you cannot interrogate the dead.

My first intention was to swim ashore below Hock Cliff regardless of the difficulty of ever regaining the opposite bank till daylight, and to leave the dinghy as it was and at anchor; but the speed with which Marrin had been swept away was terrifying and only my hand on the gunwale prevented me from following. So I climbed on board, shipping a good deal of water, and started the engine. It would not hold us against the tide but allowed me to ease the boat into the shore of the Noose not too far down. Then I gave it a shove and sent it spinning on its way to the sea. I wished there to be no awkward mystery about Marrin's death. More charitably, I hoped the dinghy might be of use to him if both were stuck on the same sandbank.

I now had to return to Bullo and recover my clothes. It was a long and wearisome plod over the Severn's special mixture of mud and sand until I reached the seawall of the Awre peninsula. I was not as cold as on the night of my escape, but it was essential not to be seen. Fortunately it was near midnight in a world emptied of men and I disturbed nothing but sheep while walking along the river to the copse and my baby pill. When I had changed I did not take the lane under the embankment, which was much too close to the cottages, but climbed directly up and over the railway. There, carrying my bundle, I must have been seen against the skyline by some gardener or fisherman trying to forecast the next day's weather by inspecting the sky instead of going to bed.

After I had crossed the main road the journey was easy enough: up a farm track and then a footpath with only a mile to go before I was safely under the oaks in one of the thickest parts of the Forest. There I became hopelessly confused, for there were rides and tracks in all directions and few visible stars to help. I should have been out till dawn if I had not crossed my usual path to Broom Lodge at a spot where I could recognize it.

I entered my den at first light, dead tired and unable to start out again even if I had wished. I ate whatever was handy and turned in. News of the major's burglary could wait. It seemed likely to fail and was futile. Even if the cauldron were proved to be of great antiquity I had no longer any hope of finding the barbaric hoard from which it had come.

In the late afternoon I set out for an evening visit to the sapling stump, keeping up my usual precautions since the hasty gulpings of the Severn might have rejected Marrin as indigestible and thrown him up on shore. I did not expect any message at all from the major. The pessimism of melancholy inclined me to believe that by this time he would have been handed over to the police or — if the commune wished to keep the scandal in the family — be locked up in disgrace pending Marrin's return.

Half an hour after I was settled in my cover a very thoughtful Denzil appeared. He had evidently made several visits in the hope of finding me.

"At last! At last!" he exclaimed.

"Did you pull it off?"

"Yes, yes!" — success no longer seemed to interest him — "Simeon has disappeared. I hope . . . I hope . . . What did you see?"

"I saw him leave Bullo Pill in his dinghy and go down on the ebb. That was all. Hasn't he come back?"

I was keeping the full story to myself. The major knew too much already and was naturally apprehensive.

"Not like him! Never missed a day!"

"He might be stranded on the opposite bank," I suggested.

"Would have telephoned. You're sure you . . . well, I mean he was all right when you left him?"

"I didn't leave him. I watched him arrive and after that all I saw was the wake of the dinghy when he started out. So you got the cauldron?"

"I could have. No trouble. No trouble at all."

"But you didn't take it?"

"Got in all right, made a mess of the place. Turned out the drawers and stole a few trinkets. But I hadn't got the key of the casket. I think Simeon keeps it on him."

"You could have taken the whole thing."

"Too heavy, Piers. Couldn't go down the drainpipe with that. I'd have had to throw it out the window. Crash! Wake somebody."

"Why the hell didn't you break it open?"

"Hadn't the heart. All that ivory work. And the bowl? What is it? We don't know. Could be . . . could be sacrilege."

It wasn't difficult to guess the cause of the inhibition. The major had no hesitation in burgling the sanctum of alchemy which he knew to be partly playacting, but when it came to violating the golden bowl his illusions, reaching all the way back to the Dark Ages and Arthur, Champion of Christendom, prevented possible sacrilege.

"Don't tell me you think that crazy murderer is the Guardian of the Grail?"

"What makes you say that?"

My remark, more a spark of exasperation than serious, had struck home. I could have disclosed the pagan ceremony I had witnessed, which was far from a proper use of the Christian Grail, but I didn't. The swings and merry-go-rounds of his own heretical funfair were too unpredictable.

"Because I don't see Marrin as Perceval. The thing was probably the favorite drinking bowl of some Saxon or Dane, or older still and the property of Nodens. Blood from his enemy or wine from his vineyard, depending on how civilized he was."

"You believe he existed before he became a god?"

"Marrin does. And you said yourself that there is always a truth behind legend."

All side issues of no immediate importance. I asked him if anyone had been in the laboratory since the burglary.

"Unlikely. I locked it all up again."

"And the broken window — has nobody noticed it?"

"I don't think so. Too high up. Eyes down. Meditation. Work."
Wearily I demanded what he had done with the swag. He
marched off into the open order of the trees, beckoning me to follow as if any speech were an indiscretion. At first he could not find
the right oak, though it was the only one which had a low branch
close to the ground. He climbed from that into a much higher
fork — he must, as he said, have been good at P.T. — and recovered a small bag well hidden by a bunch of mistletoe.

"There you are! Up to you now!"

An embarrassment. He should have left it up in the mistletoe. But he gave me no chance, and there was I with the proceeds
of a pointless burglary which had been the major's idea anyway.

I had no doubt that Marrin was drowned. Thus there was no
object — at any rate for the moment — in remaining dead. What I
had to do in order to get the full facts and keep in touch with developments was to reappear at Broom Lodge as the spontaneous and
sympathetic visitor. So I rearranged my den to look as if some
tramp had lived there in the past but not recently, and took the last
train back to London. Next day, bathed, respectable and dressed
with conventional casualness I drove down to the Forest and paid a
casual call at Broom Lodge as if on my way to South Wales. The
place was disorganized, the workshops silent, and groups hanging
about like listless bees without a queen.

Elsa met me at the front door and told me that her uncle was
dead.

"His body was found yesterday afternoon caught in a salmon
weir below Purton. The police telephoned us at once."

"Good God! One of his fishing expeditions?"

"I think so. He drove away the night before last without telling
anybody, and I know it's the river when he does that. It looks as if
he must have fallen in. He wasn't dressed for a dive. I told the police to make inquiries at Bullo Pill. And, Piers, we've had a burglary. The police discovered it. All the drawers in the lab had been
turned out and I don't know quite what is missing except that he
stole the golden bowl."

My face must have shown my surprise and horror, but under the circumstances both were natural enough. Had the major lied to me, or, more likely, had one of the damned druidicals slipped in and pinched the sacred totem for the use of the sect?

"Casket and all?" I asked.

"He just smashed the casket and took it. And the police have come back again this morning. They are wondering if there couldn't be some connection between Simeon's death and the burglary."

There could indeed be. Burglar knows Marrin is out and that the lab will be empty. Obvious and what actually happened. Alternatively and much worse, burglar pushes Marrin into the river to be sure that he can't interrupt and then returns to Broom Lodge for the gold.

"The dinghy was picked up by a coaster coming into Sharpness," she went on. "His diving stuff in its case was on board. People at Bullo confirmed to the police that his boat was missing and said that he must have taken it out the night before last. And somebody saw a man about midnight carrying a bundle and scrambling up the railway embankment instead of taking the lane past the cottages. That looks queer, doesn't it?"

I asked her what would happen now and if Broom Lodge could carry on.

"I suppose so. I know he's left everything to the commune."

"And nothing to you?"

"I don't want anything. It's all so uncertain. Who owns what? Think of lawyers and the Revenue trying to find out where an alchemist got his gold!"

She had a moment of hysteria, laughing and sobbing at the same time.

"But, my darling, you know he wasn't one."

"I don't! He was so many things."

I asked if the major was about. I hoped he wasn't. I could imagine him complicating the whole situation with military or esoteric incoherencies.

"No, I hear he's spending his time praying in Blakeney church.

The return of the prodigal I suppose, now that poor, deluded Simeon isn't here to influence him. I think he'll go home."

A voice materialized from behind us where there had been nobody.

"Excuse me, Miss Marrin! I wonder if I might have a word with this gentleman."

A detective sergeant in plain clothes identified himself. This, I thought, could be the end, but it was only a beginning. He had been informed that the late Mr. Marrin had taken me diving with him at the Guscar Rocks. Could I tell him how experienced he seemed and what his practice was? Did he always change in his dinghy, or on the night of his death would he have been crossing the river with the intention of going in off the land somewhere on the other side?

I found it easy and natural to tell him the little I knew: that I had the impression he always went in off the land and that unless his boat was fairly large and stable he would not have dived from it and returned to it.

Then he turned to the experiment in salmon fishing, of which he had heard from the commune, and to later night dives which he gathered Mr. Marrin seldom spoke of because they had some religious meaning for him. Perhaps I could explain that. The sergeant was evidently relieved to have a chance of talking to a sane outsider.

I made what sense I could of it all, telling him that the commune believed in the transmigration of souls, that service to mankind in this life was what would be remembered in the next and that they trained themselves in simple crafts which could be useful at some future time when the survivors of inevitable disaster — disease, starvation or atomic pollution — had reverted to the same state as Neolithic man.

To my surprise he thought there might be something in it.

"Making a bloody mess of our world we are, Mr. Colet, and that's a fact. But what has it got to do with underwater fishing?"

"I think you'd be on safe ground in describing Mr. Marrin as a keen naturalist," I said, "but with an original point of view of his

75]

own. He was not interested in description or discovery, but what you and I and the fish have in common. All life is one and that sort of thing."

"Thank you very much, Mr. Colet. You make it all much clearer than those poor ... er, yes. And I can't get anything very exact about the missing objects."

"Which of them?" I asked, feeling that I was now accepted as a friend and confidant of the late Simeon Marrin.

"Some small objects of gold. And according to members of the commune a golden bowl of great value. It was in a casket which was smashed."

"Oh, he made them. That was his hobby. He wasn't a very experienced goldsmith but he enjoyed it. He once told me that his work had only the value of the gold."

"You don't know, I suppose, where he bought it?"

I replied that I had never asked him, and then thought that I ought to try to conform to the evasive and contradictory answers which he would have gotten from the more credulous members of the commune.

"I've heard some nonsense about mining and also that he had a process for extracting gold from seawater."

"Is that possible?"

"Yes, but I believe it would cost far more to extract than its worth."

"So it would not be possible in his laboratory?"

"No. If you're thinking of all that lead, mercury and other stuff in the lab I'm pretty sure it was for experiments with alloys."

"Would you say it was widely known that he had so much gold on the premises?"

"I don't know. Not widely, I should think. But you had better ask the members of the commune that. They gave hospitality freely. It looks to me as if someone knew he had fallen out of his boat and drowned and then made a dash across country to get at the gold."

"He may not have been drowned, sir. It could have been a blow at the back of the skull which killed him."

I wondered whether an autopsy could tell whether he drowned after being knocked out by the blow and falling in, or whether it came by accident while he was still just alive. There couldn't, I think, be conclusive evidence either way after eighteen hours at the mercy of the tide and tangling with a salmon weir.

I could guess what had happened. Marrin had tumbled out of the dinghy, rigid with terror, and though the lias below Hock Cliff is softish rock there are chunks of hard stone imbedded in it. If he had crashed his head on one, that accounted for the swiftness with which the ebb had carried his body away.

"And where can we find you, Mr. Colet, if there is any point on which we think you might be able to help us?"

I gave him my London address, saying that I was on my way to South Wales but would be keeping in touch with Miss Marrin since I should like to be present at the funeral.

Elsa had disappeared while we were talking and I now went to find her. She seemed to be distraught rather than mourning her uncle and begged me to keep in touch with her. I promised to do so. Her last words as I returned to my car were a whisper:

"Dear, dear Piers, get me out of here!"

I shall, and please God I shall not be taken away from you or you from me.

I drove away to the silent brink of the Severn, rippling with the wind against the tide, and considered my position. If the police ever began to suspect me, they would then want to know where I was staying after I left Broom Lodge and where I was on the night that Marrin died. I can't account for my movements and if I were a magistrate I should commit for trial this now elegant economist with his pretended interest in ancient history by which he gained the confidence of the late Simeon Marrin. But, after all, why should the police investigate my movements? I was a respected and respectable academic, the understanding friend of the commune and eager to help them.

So, with luck, it should appear quite natural if I resumed occasional appearances at Broom Lodge as a casual visitor. That allowed me to keep our love alive and to whisk Elsa out of there if the commune dissolved into anarchy. Meanwhile she could relay to me as much as the police chose to tell her.

The only disquieting thought was that my life and liberty depended on the major, who alone knew of my secret movements. So long as he stayed in the district I had to keep in close touch with him. He was an admirable burglar — provided that he had worn gloves as he intended — but he was not a man to talk himself out of trouble.

So there it was! I still had no clue to the site of the hoard which Marrin had been robbing while putting up his smoke screen of alchemy, apart from the very valuable information that it was on the other side of the river. Also it was essential to get the cauldron out of the hands of the tonsured long enough for an expert examination. That should not be impossible. For example, there might well be an In Memoriam ceremony for Marrin which I could surprise. But if the wolf were to pad through the darkness behind those unsuspecting druidicals, the den was indispensable as his headquarters.

It was then that a compromise occurred to me: to adopt a dual personality. Outwardly I should remain the economist attracted by Elsa, which would explain visits to Broom Lodge. At the same time and chiefly at night I should be the secret investigator on the part of history and the public. Personality No. 1 would be Piers Colet, an innocent bystander whose life of learning and travel had been beyond reproach. Personality No. 2 would be the wolf hidden in its forest den, ready to track and to spring.

So I have returned to the den, where the major's damned bag of golden bits and pieces is safely hidden. Elsewhere I keep the diving equipment together with a suitcase containing the clothes of Personality No. 1. Details of changing back to him have proved more difficult than I foresaw — for example, access to my car, neatness, telephoning Elsa supposedly from South Wales. Meanwhile I have been out every night — without any result — and during the day have written this simple and factual account of the events leading to Simeon Marrin's death which, if it should ever have to be used in my defense, will not, I hope, be rejected as an ingenious fabrication. As I have said, his death was the last thing I wanted. What I do want is to recover the cauldron and manage a clear run so that I can take it to the British Museum for a verdict. After that can begin the search for what remains of Marrin's find.

*PART*

All this and no nearer to the source of the gold! A week ago I was beginning to feel that Personality No. 2 and his precious den were quite unnecessarily dramatic, that there was nothing to prevent me from carrying off Elsa to London and that the site of the burial where Marrin had found the bowl might be better investigated by archaeologists who were personal friends and knew me well enough to accept as much of my story as I chose to tell them.

But circumstances took over, such simple circumstances starting from my curiosity about charcoal and leading so rapidly to —well, among other things, another unfortunate accident. But I can't deny that I intended the merciless hunting and haunting of these druidicals and that Elsa's mention of sacrifice merely increased my contempt for them.

Her uncle had kept her very much in the dark. After all, church servants have more to do with dusting the pews than with doctrine. She thinks that Uncle Simeon joined this esoteric sect before Broom Lodge came into being and that it was to the sect that its former owner, the retired and heretical parson, left the place. The handful of druidicals was too small to run it, so Marrin hit on the fashionable idea of a working commune, the members of which would be sympathetic to reincarnation, meditation and fairly unorthodox Buddhism, and easily take him as their guru. These industrious and estimable innocents accepted that there was a higher state of spirituality into which one might be initiated when found worthy, but few were interested. I see an almost exact parallel, not religious but financial, in the machinations of a company promoter who registers a small company with nominal capital destined to act as the majority shareholder in a much larger concern to which an unsuspecting public has contributed the funds.

The druidicals had of course nothing in common with the Order of Druids which makes a nuisance of itself at Stonehenge and has no more to do with the original Druids than the Royal and Ancient Order of Buffalo has to do with buffalo. Their religion was the real goods, so far as it could be constructed, combining the little we know of the supposed wisdom of the Celtic priesthood, reincarnation and all, with the natural animism of forest dwellers. Spirits were everywhere — under the earth, under the trees, under the tides of the Severn — and at the command of man if approached with the proper respectful mumbo jumbo. Among them could be the spirit of a hero, not unlike a Greco-Roman god, who had done great service to his fellows and remained in race memory. Above the divine spirits were archangels and above them, at the point where all religions merge, the absolute and eternal.

Some of this I had from the major, who informed me that many of the beliefs could be contained within the early Christian heresy of Gnosticism. He was shocked by his old friend Simeon, but not as exasperated as an agnostic snorting at so much nonsense. After all, the Church accepts or did once accept angels and evil spirits, though I rather think it draws the line at spirits who are neither one nor the other, invisibly leading happy lives of their own.

When he did not turn up at Marrin's funeral I hoped that the only reason was religious objection to the possible rites of sending the defunct on to godhead; but it could be that he was suffering from a sense of guilt and on the verge of confession. I called his home number to see if he was there. His housekeeper — no doubt of canonical age — said that so far as she knew he was still at

Broom Lodge. So it seemed likely that my knight-errant from the Horse Guards had gone off on pilgrimage to Glastonbury or some other Arthurian site, meditating on stirrups or the Grail.

Myself I did attend the funeral: a meeting of the whole commune with the usual speeches and unusual prayers. Marrin was then carted off and conventionally cremated without any further service at all. Let him rest in peace. He was a superb craftsman. The police had raised no objection to cremation, so I could hope that the fracture of the back of his skull had been ascribed to natural causes for the time being. Microscopic examination may have shown fragments of identifiable rock.

So long as I avoided curiosity and possible suspicion by showing myself too often in the neighborhood of Broom Lodge there was no reason why Personality No. 1 should not move freely, apart from the difficulty of changing into him; nor was Elsa accountable to anyone for her absences. So a luxurious double room was booked at Thornbury, safely across the river, for Mr. and Mrs. Piers Colet and for the first time we were free to make love with abandon, sleep in each other's arms, eat and drink and laugh together. "Get me out of here!" she had begged me immediately after her uncle's death, but now she was hesitant, and all she would say in answer to my insistence was "Wait, my darling!" I supposed that she was moved by a reluctant feeling of duty to the commune. But we were not yet so accustomed to each other that I could make a good shot at the cause of her occasional reticence.

While we were walking in the hotel garden, putting off as long as possible the moment of parting, she suddenly asked me:

"Why do they go to Wigpool?"

"I think for iron ore, unless they are just having fun underground."

"It couldn't be for iron," she said. "Uncle Simeon bought the supplies for the blacksmith's shop. It's all full of rods and plates already."

"But all the same it could be for the ore."

In one way Marrin was no fraud. It was all very well to learn to handle iron, but that scanty remnant of humanity reborn into the

Neolithic culture which he foresaw, would not know how to get the raw material.

"I'm prepared to bet anything that they are mining the iron ore with pick and shovel," I said, "and somewhere in the Forest are smelting it with coal. Or better! Smelting it with charcoal on the off chance that our descendants think coal is only useful for chucking at chickens."

"Well, they do try to smelt it."

"At Broom Lodge?"

"No. Somewhere in the Forest. I remember he had some leaflets printed inviting schoolchildren to watch a demonstration. It seemed quite innocent and good propaganda for the commune. I did wonder if it had anything to do with their silly sacred ingots, but they come from Wigpool, I think."

"What sacred ingots?"

"They are on a table by the entrance to the lab, and the initiates bless them when they pass. I wish I knew what they are doing at Wigpool."

"Easy! I'll find out and tell you."

"But if they find you hanging about?"

"They won't. Don't you bother!"

"Piers, where are you living?"

"You know I am always traveling."

"Just one hotel to another?"

"That's it."

"And all of them smell of coal?"

"Darling, what did you say to me? Wait!"

"Don't take risks, Piers!"

"In search of what? The golden cauldron?"

"You were taking risks long before that disappeared."

"Diving with your uncle?"

"Where's his second suit, Piers?"

"Offered to Nodens, I expect."

"They do offer things to somebody," Elsa said.

"How do you know?"

"Piers dear, I don't know how I know. I watch their faces as I've watched yours. And I wonder. And when things are missing I ask questions and get answers I don't believe."

"What sort of things?"

"Animals and flowers and . . . diving suits?"

"And you think the altar is at Wigpool? Then they have the cauldron there!"

"They might have. But, Piers, please, no!"

When we had gone our separate ways, I recrossed the Severn Bridge and left my car in a public parking lot at Chepstow. With such a number of tourists on their way to and from South Wales or the valley of the Wye the lot was always full of cars, and mine was safely lost among them. In any case no one at Broom Lodge except Elsa knew its number. I then took a bus into the Forest and so by footpaths across country to my den.

I had been underrating Elsa's powers of observation, partly because she was so young, partly for her lack of interest in the religious aspects of Broom Lodge. But she was ageless woman all through, sensitive to discordancies of collective mood or individual deviations from the norm, even if as slight as a change of wind in woodland. She was content to notice without seeking, as I would, at once to explain.

Nodens had turned up several times as if he were a patron saint of the colony. Natural enough. His temple dominates the Severn and the Forest, and I am surprised that early British bishops did not build a church on the hill top and dedicate it to Saint Nodentius, martyr and miner, whose head was cut off by the prefect of the port, kippered in salmon oil and thereafter able to heal the sick.

In fact the inscriptions show that he was greatly honored by the Romans, who always recognized a useful god when they saw one. The river and the Forest were his and his specialties were healing and finding lost property.

Writing those words has suddenly illuminated that curious incident of the lost watch. Carver was perhaps not looking up to heaven to see if there was a magpie in the branches above him; he could have been sending up a prayer of thanks to Nodens.

I have some sympathy for what was genuine in Marrin. Nodens

could well have been an ancestral hero, older than Romans or Celts, who in time became a god. It's a pleasant thought (for which I have no evidence whatever) that he might have been the marine engineer who planned the voyage of the great stones of Stonehenge all the way around Wales, across the Severn estuary and up the Avon.

Such practical details of life in the past fascinated Marrin as they do me. That is why we got on easily together. It is also why he desperately wanted me out of the way. Our interests were close enough — though his crazily extended from past into the future — for him to be afraid that my specialized knowledge might expose the secret of how he financed his colony.

The smelting of iron ore seemed a good point at which to start investigation. So next day I decided to be a private eye and play the major's game of calling at pubs on the northern side of the Forest. In order to appear businesslike I used my car and Personality 1, carrying 2's outfit in case of need. What I wanted to know was where I could buy a quantity of charcoal. At the big factory, I was told, which supplied the chemical industry. But did anybody still burn charcoal by the old method? Yes, two enterprising ex-miners were hard at it and coining money, though you wouldn't think it to look at 'em. They had developed a new and profitable market: the suburbs of the larger towns within easy reach where families had fallen for the new craze of outdoor barbecues.

And so to the fairy-tale scene of a charcoal burner. The pyramid of wood smoldered under its beehive cover of turf and clay, pouring out trickles of smoke from the vent holes. Alongside the oven were stacks of beech and oak, and a hut where one of the partners was always on duty day and night. Apparently a charcoal pit is more nuisance than a baby. It must be inspected every two hours in case it bursts into flame; and there is only one way to build the shallow pit which contains the beehive. That is to learn it from your father who learned it from his father.

All this the burner on duty, evidently pleased to have company, told me, a cheerful grin splitting his black-dusted face. I arrived at the point which interested me by saying that I couldn't understand how charcoal could produce enough heat to melt iron from the ore, and got the most surprising answer.

"Cor! Shouldn't a believed it meself! But now 'ee canst go see it done. Customers of mine they are. 'Eathen Mohammedans, I'm told, but no 'arm in 'em. All live together and do everything as it ain't done no more. Now, if 'ee 'urries — " He pulled out a printed sheet from his pocket and consulted it. "Aye, there's frying to-day! Nip on down to Flaxley Woods, and you'll catch 'em at it twixt road and stream."

I knew exactly where he meant and hurried, after changing in the car to Personality 2. Car and 2 were not supposed to be seen together but the risk was small and any future developments seemed likely to call for No. 2 and his feet. Not far off the road was a quarter circle of low cliff left by ancient diggings, and below it open grass where time and the rains had smoothed spoil from the mine into a bumpy amphitheater. There a furnace had been built of uncut stones mortared with clay. Near it was standing the Broom Lodge van containing sacks of charcoal.

A huge pair of bellows projected from the bottom of the kiln, worked by Raeburn stripped to the waist with the sweat pouring down his chest. Ballard was holding a mold in tongs, about to catch the drip from the furnace. Three small groups were watching: one of children and a schoolmaster, another of passersby and a third of four middle-aged and scholarly-looking men who might have been social historians or assistant directors of a folk museum.

They were getting their iron on the spot. At the back of the hollow and at the foot of the low cliff a band of ore showed plainly which probably petered out too soon to have been of interest to a miner. A better demonstration for schoolchildren I cannot imagine. There was the whole process from the rock to the ingot.

One question, however, puzzled me. The homemade ingots were far from commonplace, but why should they be sacred? I guessed at a very tentative answer. The whole setup could be a most ingenious blind, like Marrin's alchemy. Since there was no easy method of smelting iron secretly, he had decided to do it publicly. It was certainly ore from the surface rock which was being extracted, but if ore from quite another source — say, their revered Wigpool — went into the furnace no onlooker would be any the wiser.

After returning to my car and driving it further between the trees I slipped back to the free show. I wanted to know what the pair of metallurgists would do when they knocked off, and I had discovered a satisfactory lair from which to watch. There miners of unknown ancestry and language had been ruthless in chasing the ore, leaving behind a landscape of miniature crags which reminded me — though the sweeping, green shelter of a great oak confirmed that I was in England — of some painting of cypresses hanging in a gray Mediterranean gorge. A branch of the oak could be reached from a sharp pinnacle of rock. I climbed the tree and between the leaves had a perfect view of the furnace and the open ground.

The spectators drifted away, the highbrows remaining to the last and asking questions of Raeburn and Ballard who were visibly impatient. Left alone, the two ran off the little remaining iron and cleared the slag. They showed no respect for the stuff and threw it into a pit. No suggestion of sacred ingots there! They then recharged the furnace with charcoal.

After satisfying themselves that no one was watching they unloaded from their truck two little bags of a powdered mineral which looked like a very shiny coal and loaded the furnace with it. Raeburn, the bellows operator, swore. That was most irreverent in view of what followed but even devout druids must be human.

"God damn the bloody tin!" he said, and turned again to the bellows.

So that was the metal of the sacred ingots. At first sight all that deception just to get a few slugs of tin seemed unnecessary. But one must remember that no smelting could be done secretly in the Forest, for the fire watchers would have been down at the first plume of smoke or the glare of the furnace by night; nor could it be done underground in the Wigpool workings. Ventilation would be a problem, especially if using charcoal.

But why not at Broom Lodge, teaching the craft to the whole

commune instead of to the inner circle only? The answer lies in the mysteries of their creed, the confusion of past and future which also attracted the major, though he managed to find it compatible with Christianity. To Marrin and his followers those earliest workable minerals, gold, tin and copper, were to be venerated, and the process of ore to ingots was more sacred still. They were reenacting the magic whereby the wizards of the tribe transmuted stones to arrowheads.

No doubt Marrin's end product was going to be bronze. Somewhere he had a source of the sacred tin. Copper he would have to buy — cheating, but it was most unlikely that he would ever find a vein of ore. Probably he was producing the alloy by means of his electric furnace, pending the elaboration of some more traditional method, to be occulted by oak grove, river mist or cave.

When dusk was beginning to fall the tin was flowing from the charcoal into the mold, enough for a small ingot of not more than three cubic inches. With ritual bows they set it aside to cool and solidify, and then retired to the cab of the truck to eat and drink.

I felt the presence of Nodens. I can only put the miracle down to him for I am not mischievous — at least not often. I decided to give these pagan puritans something to think about: an ingot really deserving veneration containing the protest of a happy Neolithic hunter against distasteful industry. Inspired by a little chip of flint exposed at the foot of my oak, neat and thin enough to be an arrowhead, though I don't think it was one, I slid down quietly from the tree, spat on it for luck, rubbed it clean with my handkerchief and dropped it into the center of the ingot so that it remained like a gem floating on the surface. Nodens was amused. Together we had created a myth. He is obviously a god whose divine nature it is to rejoice in the improbable. A finder of lost property could be nothing else, especially if he had stolen it in the first place.

When the two returned, their behavior was even more exaggerated than I expected. They got the hunter's message all right. After silent prayer they fetched a black velvet cushion from the truck and with the tongs reverently placed the ingot upon it. When the cushion naturally began to smoke they recovered common sense and looked around for a safe high altar upon which the ingot might be put, setting it temporarily on the flat top of the very pinnacle from which I had climbed my oak. It astounds me how the ultrapious of any religion will always choose some esoteric explanation of the otherwise inexplicable rather than ascribe it to human intervention. And that is a pity because it merely provides ammunition for those who scoff at the possibility of any unknown source of power.

The pair stood by their truck discussing whether they should leave the ingot in the impressive position where it was or carry it back to Brother Evans. They decided on Brother Evans. Lord help the community, I thought, if that pretentious fool had succeeded Marrin! The inner circle might accept him as High Priest, but I doubted if the main body of honest and innocent colonists would take his orders.

"He'll still be up there," one of them said.

I sneaked hastily back to my car and took the main road through the Forest which they, too, would have to follow unless — unlikely — they meant to go down to the river. At a crossroads some four miles away I had a good chance of discovering where "up there" was. They would turn left for Broom Lodge and right for Wigpool. If they drove straight on it would be to an unknown destination, and I dared not follow too closely.

I got away just ahead of them and parked in cover by the crossroads. They turned right. I gave them five minutes and cautiously circled Wigpool Common until I was approaching the Bailey Rock — or where I believed it to be, for the major's report of his expedition had merely mentioned it. I could not find any good hiding place for the car and finally left it parked among others outside a Methodist chapel where some fete or committee meeting was in progress. Then I set out on foot.

Narrow lanes and open tracks seemed to lead in all directions. My chief fear was that the truck would find me, not I the truck. It was just after lighting-up time and I could only hope that the druidicals were good citizens and that the headlights of their oncoming truck would give enough warning for me to dive into the nearest ditch. I need not have bothered. This last finger of the Forest, pointing north, was so remote that I saw no wheeled vehicle whatever.

However, I did see tire tracks when I was crossing an open field. Since they were recent and led to a copse where there was no gate I was interested. They could of course have been made by a farmer inspecting his fences but he had neither returned nor driven off to either side and apparently had gone on into the copse. In that case he might have cut the wire and replaced it. Close examination showed that he had, and inefficiently — odder and odder and unfarmerlike unless he had gone in to haul out timber. There was no sign of that, so I climbed the barbed-wire fence —making my hard-worn trousers more disreputable than ever —and followed the tracks. They led me into a thicket of bramble and decaying pine trees, leaning or uprooted by the wind, and there was the major's ancient Humber.

It looked very much as if Brother Evans had the same reactions as Marrin when threatened. Around the forlorn and friendly old car there was no sign of life except swooping bats. A detective no doubt would have come up with a dozen deductions, but the only one I could make was that the car must be at a safe distance from the shaft where the "geologists" were prospecting with the full knowledge of the local villagers.

Prospecting for what? For gold the major had thought at first. But that I was sure was nonsense. I myself had suggested that they were communing with spirits of the earth, which seemed to me quite a likely lunacy if there was a black lake somewhere underground. The answer now was more prosaic. They were searching for tin among the remaining pockets of iron in a mine long since deserted.

I reckoned that it was no good looking for the truck, which must have left long since if Brother Evans had been driven back to the site of the furnace to inspect and collect the fabulous ingot, so my only hope was to find the shaft though it was nearly dark. I retraced my steps to the Bailey Rock and started again to explore the open country to the north of it, feeling that I had been too obsessed by the shadowy forest. I could find no recent heaps of spoil nor any hut. But there need not be either. A hole in a slope or low cliff would be enough. I remembered such a slope where half an hour earlier I had tripped over rusty bits of machinery overgrown by long grass. A small mine must have once been thereabouts, so I followed the foot of the slope.

I nearly walked slap into a sentry. He was sitting on a pile of pit props and away to his left was a jagged patch of black which had to be the entrance to the shaft. He heard me, but by the time he had got to his feet and started to flash a torch around I was lying flat in cover. A few sheep were sleeping not far off and I think he must have assumed that the slight noise was due to one of them, for he settled back on his pit props and lit a pipe. Working around him on lower ground I crossed the wheel marks of traffic coming and going on a rough lane, which confirmed that I was in the right place. So I crawled up the slope and made myself comfortable on the grass above the sentry, prepared to wait until something happened. As usual I was hungry, having had nothing since a breakfast of scraps in the den, but food could wait. By way of charcoal and schoolchildren I was on the scent of the golden cauldron. This was where it was, stolen by Evans & Co. before Marrin's executors could get at it and now presiding over their futile ceremonies when it ought to be on a table in the British Museum with experts in committee around it to decide its date and provenance.

The truck returned with Evans, Raeburn and Ballard. They picked up the sentry and drove off after a short conversation which I was not near enough to overhear. A light drizzle had drifted into the Forest from the Welsh mountains and under the low cloud darkness and silence were absolute. I came down to the mouth of the shaft and walked along the passage until I was stopped by a wall of solid timbers reinforced by bands of iron, which had evidently been in place for years, presumably to keep out adventurous children. I could find no opening in the sides of the shaft offering a way around it and would have assumed that I was in the wrong place if it had not been for the scatter of pit props. Depressed by the wet mist and the difficulty of finding any concealed entrance in broken ground and thick night I gave up and tried to return to the Methodist chapel and my car. Tried, I write — for the country was like an open maze in which the shortest apparent route led nowhere and the longest way round was usually right. When I slumped into the driving seat I was tired out and damned if I was going all the way to the Chepstow parking lot.

I left the car on a forest track close under my hill and staggered shivering up to the den with the bag containing the tweed suit of that sane and ordinary economist Personality No. 1. My own supplies of alcohol were finished. So was the major's whisky. But after I stripped off my soaking clothes his magnificent rug enabled me to get some tepid sleep with knees to chest. I hoped that he at least was fed and warm and dreaming of the Grail. It seemed unlikely. Remembering the Box Rock, I was obsessed by the thought of the black pool reported to be at the bottom of the workings.

In the morning I spread out No. 2 outfit to dry though I could not see how the devil it was going to when even the midday sun hesitated to enter my safe but gloomy home. Then I drove into Chepstow and consumed an immense breakfast at the hotel. Resting in the lounge afterward and reviewing the events of the night, the pile of pit props came to mind. I had not looked at them closely, but memory behind the eyes recalled ragged ends in all and a deep split in one. Now surely Marrin would have bought new and trustworthy props? He could well afford them and he was always thorough. The pile of props could be another of his ingenious frauds. That man ought never to have been a professional prophet. He'd have been famous as a designer of sets for the National Theatre. Under the pile, easily to be moved and rearranged, could be an entrance which bypassed the barrier.

I had at once to find the major if only to relieve my own anxiety. Since my opponents were armed with religion rather than reason it was also essential to protect Elsa against incalculable reactions. I telephoned her at the estate office insisting again that she should leave Broom Lodge at once and hand over her life to me as lover or husband or whatever she liked. She murmured that husband would do very well but then she seemed anxious, depressed and obstinate. Land and workshops were running normally with the colonists as diligent as ever, but naturally there were questions on the minor day-to-day issues of policy and finance. Her uncle used to settle them all decisively and with common sense and now the commune expected her to advise them. The man Evans had quietly taken over religious leadership but when it came to the practical running of the colony he left it to the various groups. Marrin's will had been short and plain enough. He had bequeathed the estate to the commune. But the commune wasn't a limited company and it wasn't a cooperative. What was it? Meanwhile the bank manager was being as helpful as he could to such a good customer.

I pitied the bank manager. Evans might be sound on ritual and reincarnation but was not a man to understand that his authority in financial matters must be legal. And he would leave an impression behind him in the manager's office that he was proud to live by barter or the begging bowl. I could only advise Elsa to refuse any responsibility and find some colonist — preferably a lawyer or accountant who had opted out of the rat race — with enough character to chair a meeting and obtain general agreement.

I thought that at last we should be able to get a line on Simeon Marrin's income and what had enriched him, but there too he had covered his tracks.

"What about the funds that he paid into the commune?" I asked.

"He drew on his private account, and they say there in London that he always paid in cash over the counter. They thought he must be some kind of a criminal until the manager here explained that he ran a monastery."

The London bank was right. A criminal he was, robbing this ancient country of invaluable evidence of its past. I had said little to Elsa on this point, allowing her to half believe in the alchemy or, failing that, in a substantial profit from his goldsmith's work. The truth might have involved me in admitting that I had been present at his death and in agonizing her with the revelation that he had tried to kill me.

"By the way, did Evans bring in a new sacred ingot this morning?" I asked.

"No. But he came in and took them all away. He said that the lab wasn't the right place for them."

I went shopping to restock the den with food, and then took the bus into the Forest and walked home. I dozed and rested through the afternoon since I might need all the endurance I had. Meanwhile the June sun was kind enough to dry last night's clothes. Before sunset I started out on the eight-mile tramp to Wigpool, taking it easy and stopping on the way for a meal. The wind, what there was of it, had gone around to the north and the night was clear and starlit.

After approaching the shaft from the back I lay down to await developments and noticed that the pile of old pit props had been arranged in something like a hollow square. That was fine. Somebody was about to go down or come out and I was prepared to watch all night for him to appear.

At last there was a quick flash of light between the timbers and a man emerged from the middle of them. I could not be sure who he was till I was closer. He turned out to be that white worm Ballard. He returned the props to their normal shape of a stack and cleared off. As I wanted to see where he had parked his car and who would pick him up, I followed him, from time to time deliberately making a little mysterious noise to bother him. I did, for he quickened his pace and started to whistle to keep up his courage. Meditation should have been enough to dispel such worldly matters. It may be harder when they are unworldly.

He walked for about half a mile along the rutted track and through a stand of splendid oaks, outliers of the Forest, until he came to a minor road where he waited. Marrin's van arrived to collect him. I could not see who was driving.

Since Ballard had carefully remade the stack it was obvious that I was going to have the night to myself and plenty of time for exploration. Considering the stories I had heard of a maze of forgotten galleries I had thought it advisable to imitate Theseus and

Ariadne and take with me a large ball of string to be used to mark my trail wherever there might be a doubt of the way back to the surface. I must admit that I did not much like such a journey unaccompanied but I was sure that both the major and the cauldron were ahead of me and either — or if possible both — would do.

As soon as I had moved the scattered props, which probably had been there for years until eyes no longer paid attention to them, I came upon four layers of them, neatly set into a square excavation. After raising these, a dark hole appeared. The diameter was very narrow, only about three feet, and my guess is that it had been the entrance to a badger sett which Marrin had excavated still further in the hope that it offered an alternative way into the workings. For the first few yards I had to crawl but then an even slope went downward, with some timbering to support the roof, until it led at a right angle into a true miner's roadway cut in rock. This was obviously the main shaft. The gallery to which badgers and Marrin had obtained access had never been intended to reach the surface and was possibly a turnout or an exploratory tunnel later abandoned.

The first question was whether to turn right uphill or left downhill along the main shaft. Right was soon eliminated. The roadway curved around, still uphill, and the beam of my torch showed the inner side of the old timber barrier; so I turned and carried on downward. The floor had been dry rock but now became wet and muddy, and it was quite believable that a stream or lake was somewhere in the depths. At a Y junction footsteps in the mud showed me which branch to take and soon I saw a faint gleam of light on the yellow, dripping wall coming from some opening on the right. I could not approach it quietly, for it was impossible to move without audible squelching. There was nothing to it but to try speed and surprise. I picked up a lump of iron ore and rushed the opening.

Sitting in a deck chair was the major reading peacefully a pocket Bible in the light of an oil lamp.

He looked up without any alarm and put down the book.

"But how kind of you to want to see how I was getting on!" he said.

My lungs were suddenly emptied of the deep breath of attack and I could only gasp:

"You're . . . you're not a prisoner?"

"I was a prisoner. But now I am here of my own free will."

I told him how I had found his hidden car, proving that he had been killed or kidnapped, and that then I had tried the Wigpool workings on the off chance that he might be there. What had happened? I asked.

"After I had performed my vigil in Blakeney church and prayed that I might be worthy — "

"Worthy of what?" I interrupted.

"Worthy of guarding the Grail."

"It is *not* the Grail," I bellowed in exasperation. "It's not a chalice or a bowl. It's a cauldron if anything."

"In Irish legend, Piers, the Grail was a cauldron."

"Well, is it down here?"

"I am sure of it."

"And you have confessed to the burglary?"

"Ashamed to say I haven't, old boy! I would have told the truth if they had asked me, but they never did."

"Then why are they holding you here?"

"I was telling you. After I had performed my vigil I went to Evans and accused him of entering the laboratory as soon as he heard of Simeon's death and taking the bowl. They showed no resentment, he and his friends. We'll talk about it, they said, and then you shall see it. So we went to Evans's room where we all had a drink. I remember walking with them to my car and then nothing else until I woke up down here. Wigpool, is it? Damned interesting, that!"

"But how could you know that the burglar hadn't taken the bowl?"

"That is what they want me to tell them."

"And what *have* you told them?"

"That when the burglar smashed the casket he was so overcome by the beauty and sanctity of the bowl that he could not bring himself to take it. And that, old boy, is as true as God's in Gloucestershire except that I didn't smash the casket."

"And what in the name of God in Gloucestershire did they think of that?"

"They wondered. They too accept that it may be the chalice which started the legend of the Grail."

"But they aren't Christians, damn it!"

"They think it is far older than Our Lord."

Well, there at least they could be right. It might be Saxon but I too thought it far older and an import from the East. I had even played with the idea that it could be more ancient still, either a part of the treasure of Nodens before he became a god, or an urn to contain his entrails in the manner of the Egyptians.

"They believe that it has been sacred from time immemorial," he went on, "that the first Britons worshipped it and the Christians after them and that both had their own myths to account for it. I do not believe that it was the Cup of the Last Supper, Piers, but I do believe that it is in some way hallowed."

"Do they know where Marrin found it?"

"No. He said that he had been led to it in a dream."

"And they believe that?"

"In two different senses. They are as subtle as theologians, Piers, when explaining the ineffable. Evans believes that Simeon was led to the hiding place of the bowl by direct inspiration: a waking rather than a sleeping dream. Some others have it that Simeon himself in a trance made it from gold transmuted by the spirit of earth. That is to say: the substance is immaterial but the shape material. A sort of immortal eternally reincarnated object. Fits the Grail, what? But too subtle."

"I'm glad they are enjoying themselves. And how long do you propose to stay here?"

"Until Evans confesses and gives the Grail into my care."

We had reached the limit of exasperating lunacy. I thought that if I could shake his delusion that the cauldron could be the Grail of legend he would break out of his complacency — Perceval if I remember was somewhat complacent too — and leave with me at once. So I told him of that In Memoriam ceremony I had witnessed which was pure midnight sorcery and as pagan and pantheistic as you could want.

"The symbol of the Cross was holy before the Crucifixion," he said. "That does not make it less holy. It means it is twice as holy. The first missionaries understood that. No, Piers, here I stay!"

"They'll put you out."

"They won't do that in case I accuse Evans of robbing the commune."

"Well, then, they'll tie a weight on you and drop you in the famous lake."

"They may, Piers, but while the bowl is here it is my duty as a servant of God and the Crown to remain."

"I'll have the police here tomorrow."

"Then I too with sorrow would enter the world of policemen. I shall confess to the burglary and tell them you have everything except the bowl. I shall also tell them how Simeon tried to kill you and that you were at Bullo Pill when he met his death."

I could have denied the lot on the grounds that the major was off his rocker, a defense which would be supported by any expert shrink — wrongly, I think, for you can be reasonably sane and yet live in a fairy tale like Don Quixote. But if the major was backed up by collective perjury on the part of the druidicals and if the police began to consider me a suspect for burglary and murder I should be in trouble. Another point, always in the back of my mind was: what would Elsa's reaction be?

"Well, stay if you must," I replied weakly. "But if you want to escape follow the footprints to the entrance. It's closed by a pile of timber which you won't be able to move from inside but it will be open at night if any of them are down here. Now settle one thing for me, Denzil! Is it here where Marrin got his gold?"

"If it is they don't know it."

"And tin?"

"Perhaps. Gold, tin and copper, Piers. The beginnings of civilization."

"Then the rest of the commune should be working with them."

"Not yet. Too sacred to the tonsured. Nothing odd about that. Same in Simeon's monastery as any other. Some are mystics, some aren't. One brother has visions, another grows lettuces. If we had a drop of Scotch down here to keep you listening, I'd explain to you the distinction between salvation by faith and salvation by works."

"Which is burglary?"

"Charity. Stopping an old friend from landing himself in jail and helping a new friend in the advancement of knowledge. Charity comes under the head of works."

There was nothing for it but to go, leaving this obstinate champion of Christendom to get on with the pagans as best he could. When I had crawled up to fresh air again I dithered. Should I leave the entrance open so that if he changed his mind he could escape, or close it so that my visit remained secret? I closed it, admitting to myself that my military saint was the stronger character.

I wandered back through the empty Forest and dark hamlets, completely puzzled. The major's story and his own reactions were — if one knew him as well as I did — plain enough, but Evans's motives were obscure. The major accuses him of taking the cauldron from the burgled laboratory as soon as he hears of Marrin's death. The major is then shut up at Wigpool until he tells them what reason he has to think that it was not the burglar who took it. He proceeds to spin them a yarn of the sanctity of the bowl being so transcendent that the burglar wouldn't touch it. A most improbable burglar. But apparently they found the explanation acceptable or pretended to.

The only answer was that the major was right: Evans did pinch the cauldron. Even so, it can never be proved. Then, if our would-be Perceval refuses to leave, why not give him a kick up the backside and send him away to his Cotswold valley to dream in peace.

Wait a minute! There ought to be something that he *can* give away. Iron ore? But everyone knows that plenty of ore remains below Wigpool, though no longer worth mining. Gold? A mining company never found any. The secret entrance? Well, they only use it at night so they certainly want to keep it secret. But the major didn't even know where he was. Give him another druidical cocktail, put him in his car somewhere in the Forest and when he wakes up all he will know is that he has been in a mine somewhere. And the secret entrance is not all that significant. Obviously they don't want ex-miners and small boys rambling around the galleries to see what they are up to and dropping in on sacrifices to the gods of the underworld.

Sacrifices. Elsa suspected them. Animals, she said. What sort of animals? Was it conceivable that they didn't draw the line at sheep? The Box Rock kept returning to my mind. Any offering to the gods should, if I remember correctly, go willingly to death. I did and so would our Perceval.

The ineffectual wolf slept and stayed in its den all the following day till the evening when it came out to reconnoiter Broom Lodge and to see if the routine of the colonists had in any way changed. I watched them return from the fields and workshops, tired and smiling. There was no way of approaching the workshops closely enough to hear any conversation but some of the routes from the fields to the house afforded sufficient cover in ditches and long grass provided the stragglers had no reason to suspect my presence. How helpless the human animal is without scent! Our eyes, looking ahead or at a companion, are not much of a safeguard unless attracted by movement.

I gathered from scraps of conversation that the commune was discontented — or not exactly discontented but feeling the way toward some kind of democratic organization. More precise was a bit of talk between a man in his late forties and his still-pretty wife who had been digging new potatoes and sorting the best for market and the rest for home consumption. It went something like this. He said:

"There's a machine for riddling spuds. Simeon was just going to buy one."

"Evans doesn't like machines."

"He's a bloody fool."

"I know, darling, but don't say so! Seven of them is a big minority."

"But the piper can't call the tune unless he's got the money."

"He will have," she said with a confidence which I think was assumed.

"Well, so long as we don't have to accept the rest of his nonsense."

"Oh, he won't ask us to do that. But are you happy, love?"

"Of course. It's still heaven when one remembers London."

And then they kissed and went on their way.

A pleasant requiem for Marrin which was well deserved. In a manner of speaking he had bribed them to support by their labor a dangerous creed but he had the skill and the leadership to make a success of it. The colonists indeed showed a lack of curiosity. They were innocent, grateful and tolerant, and I'd call the lack of curiosity healthy. They were like, let's say, receivers of stolen goods at second or third hand, trustfully buying and selling them with nothing on their conscience.

I caught a glimpse of Elsa in the distance, but could not approach her as I was. She was wearing her delightful abbess gown — I am sure it was to give herself more authority — and appeared to be directing or criticizing some operation at the door of the smokehouse. I felt she might be unwise. She too believed that she was up against nothing more sinister than religious eccentricities. I decided to call on her in the morning, driving openly up to Broom Lodge as Personality No. 1. I was uncertain whether I should tell her of the fate of the major or not. The first necessity was to get her out of there.

Next day I found Elsa wandering aimlessly about the garden and recognized in her the same vague worry, the same unwillingness to commit herself, that I felt during our idyllic stay at Thornbury. She wouldn't leave and she wouldn't stay. Eventually she snapped at me that the police had been back, asking her how long it was between the time she was told on the telephone of her uncle's death and the time she left the office to give the news to the commune.

"But why?"

"I think because someone could have found out the burglary before the police did."

"They are right, Evans or one of them did, and took the cauldron."

She asked me how I knew, and I told her of my visit to the Wigpool mine and how I found the major insisting that the cauldron was the Grail and that he wouldn't leave the mine until he had it.

"But what made him think the burglar didn't take it?"

That put me on the spot. I was not going to admit that we had arranged the burglary in order to carry the thing up to London for expert opinion.

"I suppose because he is close enough to those damned druidicals to understand them. He says they believe it so holy that nothing would have stopped them from taking it for their rites if they had a chance. You don't know half of their futilities."

To draw her attention away from that awkward question I gave her the story of how her mention of the public demonstration of smelting had set me on the way to discovering that the sacred ingots were of tin and, one thing leading to another, how I had found the major's car; as an example of inner-circle superstitions I told her of the preposterous behavior of Ballard and Raeburn when I dropped a flake of flint into the ingot.

She heard me out but I could see her mind was elsewhere.

"Why did they kidnap the major?" she asked.

"Because he accused Evans of stealing the bowl."

"What made him think the burglar didn't take it?" she repeated.

"Well, I've given you the best explanation I can. He has an idea that the burglar was struck dumb by its beauty."

"Did he say anything about footprints?"

"No. What footprints?"

"I told you. The police think someone could have found out about the burglary before they did and taken the bowl."

"But what's it got to do with footprints?"

"The burglar upset a jar of sulfur or something and stepped in it and they found bits of the casket on top of the footprints instead of under them."

I saw the point but it did not seem very solid evidence. The major had possibly been quite glad to leave mucky footprints all over the place from which his movements could be traced. But supposing the feet approached the curtained shelf, perhaps stood still in front of it and then went straight to the window and down the drainpipe, any detective would wonder how the remains of the casket came to be on top of the footprints.

"It doesn't matter. The police aren't going to accuse you, my darling."

"But I did steal the bowl and I did smash the casket."

She burst into tears and I tried to comfort her. I didn't give a damn if she had the golden cauldron. I was delighted. At last I was free to take it away and have it examined.

"When I heard of his death," she said, clinging to me and still sobbing, "the first thing I did was to get the key from his desk and unlock the lab and see if there was any message for me or the commune or anything. And then I saw the place had been burgled and the casket was still there. I thought it must be somebody in the commune. Any of them could have taken the keys from his desk. And then I thought: he's missed the bowl and he shan't have it. It's mine. So I smashed the casket at the hinge and took the bowl and then I smashed the casket some more. But afterward I felt so guilty. All the time we were together I felt guilty."

"Nonsense! You were his nearest relative."

I might have been a little shocked if I had not known her sudden impulses, which were youthful, and the determination of her character, which was not. Her act had not been cold-blooded. It was a mixture of sorrow and exasperation, to which, as I was to see a moment later, could be added suspicion.

"Where is it?" I asked.

"I put it in the wastepaper basket and covered it up, and later I hid it in the Forest. Piers, I don't even know if it's really gold, only that it's mysterious and beautiful and he made it."

I said that, if he did, it was by melting down something else, of far greater value.

"What happened, I am sure, was that he discovered an ancient treasure buried somewhere near the bank of the Severn. That was when he put out the story of the win on the football pools. He really got the funds from Broom Lodge by melting down the gold and remaking it so that the origin could never be recognized. He spared the cauldron because it was so splendid and made such a mystery of it for his followers that they believed it had some occult power. So does that crazy major."

"You should never have gone down at Wigpool," she cried. "And it's all my fault! I told you they could be dangerous."

To stop her blaming herself I said that I couldn't take them seriously, and I told her about the In Memoriam service I had attended — certainly impressive but childish mumbo jumbo all the same.

"Who was dead?" she asked.

"Nobody that I know of."

"Then why do you call it In Memoriam?"

"Well, it looked like it," I answered weakly. "Evans's grand-mother perhaps."

"That night when you left us — I know Uncle Simeon drove away with two diving suits and came back with one."

"I forgot to give it back to him."

"So you were separated."

"Yes, he was going back to Broom Lodge, and I wasn't."

"Then he left before you came out of the river."

"Elsa dear, you know how unaccountable he was."

"And that's why you wouldn't come back to us and lived in the Forest!"

"In a way, I had to know what he had found. A burial? Saxon? Roman? Or something far earlier and quite unknown to history? The tomb of Nodens if he ever was a real person? To my way of thinking it was an unspeakable crime to keep secret such a discovery and perhaps destroy it. But to your uncle it was a gift of the gods which allowed him to keep his colony running — literally a gift of the gods, he may have thought."

"He was a wonderful craftsman," Elsa said doubtfully.

"Superb! I know. The major tells me that Evans & Co. have it that he was divinely inspired. But if he did make the cauldron, where did he get the gold?"

"For heaven's sake leave it alone now! What does it all matter to us two, my darling?"

"Nothing, when you say so. But first I must get the major out of there. You see that."

"Will he come?"

"Yes, if I give him my word that you, not those fanatics, have the Grail."

I assured her that there was no need to worry about me, saying that I could go down and come up again in daylight that very afternoon provided that our precious druidicals were all at honest work and that the pile of pit props was undisturbed. She was not content and, as if she could foresee dangers which I could not, wanted me to describe the slope, the entrance, the blocked gate, the lot. She said that I ought to be accompanied by the police or at least to let them know. I pointed out that the police were the last people we wanted to talk to. It would take longer to explain the motives of all concerned than to get the major out and away, and there were details about which the police would quickly see that we didn't want to talk.

"I'll get on with it at once," I said. "After lunch check that the seven druidicals have all gone off to work, especially Evans. As soon as they are all safely occupied, go out at the back and wave a tablecloth. Then I'll start off."

I had to promise to come straight back to her when it was all over. I told her that it was hard to give a definite time. I might have to wait in cover to make sure there was no one about. Denzil might decide to lecture me on faith and works before making up his mind. And I should have to play our return by ear. I suggested that she should stay in the office from six o'clock on and I would telephone her if all was well. If I failed to call her, I would meet her about seven-thirty at a spot which I would show her.

"If you don't telephone and don't turn up, I'm going to the police," she said.

I had no objection. If I didn't turn up by seven-thirty it could mean that I wasn't going to turn up at all. Her vague fears had made me take this simple expedition rather more seriously. I remembered that I had only been as far as the major's temporary bed-sitting-room and did not know what was in the darkness beyond. The ingenuities of the late Simeon Marrin were not to be despised.

I showed her where she was to meet me — the lair in the foxgloves from which I had kept watch on the back of Broom Lodge — and settled down there to eat some sandwiches and wait for her signal.

A little after three the tablecloth was waved — a long enough wait to show me that she had made a thorough check of suspects and occupations. I returned to the car, changed to the shabbier Personality No. 1 and drove off to Wigpool. No tea and buns were being served at the Methodist Chapel and there were no cars outside, so I had to look for some other discreet parking place, not too far away. I passed no one in my walk to the rising ground above the shaft, but when I lay down and looked over the edge, I found that a tractor was traveling back and forth over the pasture between slope and woodland cutting thistles, and that I should be in full view of the driver when I dismantled the pile of pit props and entered the shaft. It was no wonder that the "geologists" only went to work when dusk had closed down work on the land and no farmhands or ex-miners full of professional curiosity were likely to stroll up and ask questions.

When the tractor drove away I cleared the pile of props and went down. All was silent. There were more tracks in the mud than on my previous visit, but only of one person coming and going. It looked as if someone had gone down to see that the obstinate major was all right, and to supply him with food and drink.

No light came from the bay he had occupied. I quickly flashed my torch on the interior, fearing the worst, and was relieved to see him sound asleep under blankets on a mattress against the wall.

I called softly:

"Denzil!"

He turned over and replied in the words of the young Samuel: "Speak, Lord!"

I said it was only me but that he could get up and gird his loins all the same.

He unrolled himself. His unshaven face, set but smiling as if I was being most courteously welcomed to the mess though they were just out of battle, made me realize that I loved the ridiculous man as Arthur might have done, had done, would do. These time travelers of imagination play the devil with one's tenses.

"You're taking a bit of risk, old boy," he said.

"None at all. I left the entrance open and we can clear out now."

"I told you . . ." he began.

"I know. But I give you my word of honor that the Grail is not here. Elsa has it."

"You have seen it?"

"Yes," I lied. "And at last we can go to the experts with it and find out how old it is and whether what you believe is possible."

"Good! And before we go we will find out what else these devil worshippers have."

He explained that when he was left alone he had explored as far as the lake — yes, there was a black lake — but could see no farther with the wretched lamp which was all the light they had allowed him. Now with my powerful torch it would be worth having another look. He knew from snatches of talk and a glimpse of Evans in a blue robe that some kind of pagan worship took place in the depths.

I doubted if there would be anything of interest except some homemade altar, but then my damned obsession with ancient economies took over. I did want to see where and how they were mining tin. Had there ever been a trade in tin from the Forest of Dean? If there had been were there already ports on the Severn

Sea before the Iron Age and the trade of the Celtic ironmasters? It was now only five o'clock. We had time in hand for a short expedition and had only to follow the footsteps until we came to the working surface, if any. The passage dipped sharply and where it ended old galleries led off to right and left. That was as far as the miners had gone before abandoning the pit. The air was still good, but probably they were getting too far from the surface for easy working and decided to exploit another of the many possible sites in the Forest where the extraction of the ore more resembled quarrying than mining.

The left-hand gallery ended at a pool. This was the water which had reflected the light of the major's lamp, but it was not a lake. Footprints led down to the edge, indicating that it could easily be waded, but there was no obvious way out on the other side. As soon as we took to the ankle-deep water we found that the pool was crescent-shaped, passing around a buttress of rock. There the cut gallery stopped and a natural cave began. No doubt prospectors or the curious had at some time gone beyond the pool and found nothing to encourage a further search for ore; so the account of what they had seen dissolved over the years into mere rumor.

When we had splashed around the corner and on to the ledge at the far side of the pool footprints occasionally reappeared. We were on an irregular terrace tilting toward the dry bed of a stream, though there was no obvious source for it except the pool itself, which presumably became a powerful springhead in winter or after heavy rain. This passage in the limestone, its roof varying in height with small stalactites hanging down, continued for about a hundred yards and suddenly opened into a spectacular high-domed cavern.

The beam of my torch searching the flattish floor at once showed up what the major anticipated. At the east end of this cathedral — I have no idea whether in fact it was east — and near the brink of the lake stood an altar. One couldn't call it a rough altar, for the craftsman Marrin had been at work. The ashlars were smooth and evenly jointed. At the back was a little dais of polished stone which could only be intended for the golden cauldron. I could visualize how the concave curve of the sides would precisely merge into the swelling curve of gold.

In front of the altar was another of Marrin's fantasies: a pattern of two concentric circles delineated by fragments of shining, white quartz cemented to the floor, the space between the circles so closely filled with figures picked out in variegated stones that one could almost call it an amateur mosaic. As well as the signs of the zodiac I recognized a number of Mithraic symbols — not surprising since all the mystery religions borrowed from each other. More sinister than this priestly play with pebbles was the surface of the altar. A channel led across it, suggesting the sacrifices Elsa had suspected. I had seen on classical altars such channels to carry away the blood. Here, too, there was a thin, dark streak descending to the ground.

Halfway down the cavern the rumored lake began. It was fed by a small stream tricking in over a smooth glacis from a recess low in the right-hand wall of the cavern and leaving the center of the lake smooth as a mirror. The black water extended under the gradually lowering roof until they nearly met. I could not look at this grinning mouth without a feeling of mistrust, not that dragons or Gwyn ap Nudd were expected suddenly to break the surface, but I was conscious of the Forest far above and that this was the sink into which the remains of rock, tree and all the two-legged, four-legged life of the light eventually filtered.

Marrin had been determined to extract some of its riches. At the edge farthest from the stream stood a windlass. Two ropes passed out from it, one dipping down into the lake while the roof of the cavern was still twenty feet above it, the other entering the slit between rock and water. An iron dredge, somewhat the shape of a cradle, hung from the windlass. This was evidently a primitive device, well within the capacity of Neolithic man, for sampling the bottom of the lake.

We decided to find out what Marrin had been fishing for, on the off chance that we might solve the problem of where he got his gold if he had not after all dug up a tomb. Because we took the brake off too casually, the heavy dredge of the upper rope hurtled to the bottom while the revolving handle nearly knocked the major into the lake. At the same time the lower rope twirled fast and irregularly around the windlass. The layout was now plain. A single rope passed over the windlass and through a pulley placed — to judge by the angle — somewhere on the bottom inside the slit of the mouth. The dredge, attached to the upper rope, was lowered and pulled out tail foremost as far as the pulley. Then the revolution of the windlass was reversed; the dredge was dragged back in close contact with the bottom and kept from rising by some frame or hoop under which rope and dredge could pass. It could then be raised and emptied into a shallow hollow in the rock, where a little silt still remained, and the contents panned or strained. I suppose that after the catch had been examined the tailings were emptied into the flow on the other side of the cave with a bucket.

We put the windlass into operation, one of us on each handle and hard work at that. The dredge brought up silt and fine gravel. No glint of gold or copper and no bones of glyptodont. Specks of iron and minerals unknown to me there were, including a few scraps of the same shiny black ore with which the furnace had been loaded and which I had heard was tin. I don't know whether it could be smelted as it was or whether it had first to be treated in Marrin's laboratory. I am sure that when he set up his dredge, using suit and Aqualung to fasten pulley and guide to the bottom, he hoped for gold — enough to give him cover for his real source. What he did find and recognized was cassiterite, the ore of tin: an unexpected and significant gift from Gwyn ap Nudd or his spirit deputy in charge of Wigpool.

We hung up the dredger exactly as we found it, and left at our ease for the entrance. It was shut. Only one of us could reach the underside of the pit props at a time, and it was impossible to move them. In case our voices could be heard outside we retired down the gallery to the major's former prison to discuss what we could do. There he seemed to have left behind him an atmosphere of tranquillity. Reasoning took over from panic.

"They don't know whether there is anybody down here or not, old boy," the major said, "because they haven't looked. The pit props now. Could have been removed by someone who had watched their comings and goings and was curious. Say, one of them goes by on some other business. Sees shaft is open. Won't go in all alone. Closes up. Runs home to report. How's that?"

It seemed unlikely. In that case we could expect the arrival in force of the regular churchgoers after dark.

"We could stand where their entrance opens out into the gallery and bonk each one over the head as he appears," I suggested.

"No right to use violence, Piers. Don't know if they have any evil intent. Why should they have? We have done them no harm."

I found it hard to believe that they would be so tolerant. After all, they had been lawless enough to kidnap the major, hide his car and shut him up just to make him confess why he did not believe that the burglar had taken the cauldron. It was probable that they had no more objection to violence than Marrin.

"Or they may think I managed to move the pile of timber and escape," the major said.

I replied that they must know damn well that it was impossible even if his strength was as the strength of ten because his heart was pure. Clearly somebody else had unblocked the entrance and might or might not have persuaded him to leave.

"But what somebody else? You?"

No, I said, not necessarily me. They had no reason to believe that I was anything but a friend of Marrin's and a casual visitor to Broom Lodge pretty certainly attracted by Elsa.

"Splendid! Hadn't remembered that! Then you can easily escape while I keep 'em occupied. That, Piers, is your duty to the Grail. Preserve it from them! You are unsuspected."

"If you can see any earthly way to escape, it's good for both of us," I replied.

"Ha! I can! My story when I am detained will be that a person — I shall not mention his name, I'll let 'em think there is a traitor among the faithful — came down to persuade me to leave. That, I am glad to say, is no lie. Two days ago you did. I refused to leave and he returned to the surface. A simple *ruse de guerre*. The enemy — if I may call them so — is advancing with no clear objective. I make him think that we are weaker than we are and his demonstration of force walks into trouble." He paused triumphantly. I was not impressed.

"But where am I while you are being detained?"

"You have swum out of sight under the lip of rock and will remain there until you can perhaps intervene."

I objected that there could be no surprise intervention since I should be seen swimming back and that meanwhile I should have died of cold. However, his idea could be improved. If I entered the mouth of the stream I could hide inside and watch developments. It was not a wide-open recess so conspicuous that it invited exploration. They might not bother with it if the major's story deceived them completely and made them sure he was alone.

"To defend the approach a long lance — " he began.

"Don't forget the stirrups, Denzil! And I thought you had ruled out violence."

"In battle against the pagan it is permissible not to turn the other cheek," he pronounced.

I doubted if the law would take that point of view. In a world less romantic than Arthur's there was no reason why pagans should not call in the police; they were not committing any crime by opening up the old Wigpool workings and erecting an altar. The major and I were the aggressors who had interfered, or could easily be made to appear so.

We went back to have another look at the blocked entrance. No sound was to be heard outside. There was nothing to do but wait. It was not so chilly as in the forbidding depths, and faint strips of light coming through the pit props seemed to give us comforting but futile contact with the warm evening outside. I remember some snatches of empty conversation and the major snoring and struggling with infidels in his sleep and an endless silence through which I myself may have dozed, for only one strip of light was left and that was gray. My watch said that it was after half past eight, when I should have been at the rendezvous with Elsa. I hoped that she would not have appealed to the police. I tried to feel confident that we could deal with the four chief druidicals provided that there were no more of them and that they were not armed with bronze spears or bows and arrows.

"And all for a quid's worth of tin!" I exclaimed.

"Metals, Piers, metals. To get their own. That was the point. And Wigpool an obvious choice."

"But which came first? Religion or metals?"

"Both. You don't understand 'em, old boy. Reenacting the past for the sake of the future — you got that much. Think of the chap who first smelted a stone and found it poured out a liquid. Put it down to his gods, didn't he? But you and I would say he had a bright idea or a lucky accident. Simeon believed that his bright ideas were inspired. You'll admit he had some reason to. And he thought there was a something which inspired, same as the chap who put it down to the gods. Underwater, underground. Searching and worshipping. That was Simeon. It paid off if he really did find the cauldron in the Severn. Paid off here, too, from his point of view."

He was silent for a moment, shaking his head in the way he had, as if one self were rejecting the arguments of another self.

"Visions of the past, old boy. Can't explain them. Not reincarnation. It's just that all time is one. You can't get out of that if you believe in eternal life. I've had visions of the past myself. Can't explain. Only last for a flash or two, but don't know what world I'm in. Give you an example. When I was taking pictures of Simeon's glyptodont, I knew at once that it was a pet. So bloody unlikely that I couldn't have invented that for myself."

"Whose pet?" I asked.

"Don't know. Like a dream. Pet and bright water. And a great blank something."

He was most impressive there in the dark. I refrained from asking him whether the pet was Arthur's and lived in the cauldron. And bright water was a pleasant dream when there was a chance that we both might finish up in black.

The first we heard of them was a dragging of timber, and we hurried down the shaft. The major entered his private recess and returned to his mattress. I ran on, crossing the pool and, when I reached the far side, taking care to shake the drips of shoes and trousers over the edge so that no fresh sparkle of water should give away my passage. For the rest of the route there were enough old footprints for my own to be muddled.

I found that the stream, after it flowed out of the side wall of the cavern and on to the lake, was shallow and ran in a bed worn down about a couple of feet below the level of the floor. In wading it I was only wet below the knees, but to enter the low mouth I had to crouch down and accept a soaking. The water, however, was not so cold as I expected, possibly descending from the divine warmth of midsummer rills down to the realm of Gwyn ap Nudd. Inside the channel Gwyn came into his own. It was riven and irregular, some of the rocks smooth with deposit and suggesting the rounded backsides of burrowing beasts, some jagged and fallen or seeming about to fall from roof and sides. Around a dark corner the passage became high and narrow. I took station just short of it, ready to retire into the cleft before a searching beam could reach me.

The party were long in arriving and had left Evans behind. There were six of them, all in white robes and each carrying a red and smoky torch: the three master druids — if that's what they called themselves — whose names I knew plus the others who had been at the forest ceremony. One of these looked thoroughly dangerous, like a heavyweight boxer who had been converted and found salvation.

The major was unaccountably absent. A good sign, I thought. They had got no more out of him, and he had no business at the hallelujah party. On the other hand, why was there a party at all since they had only come down to find out how and by whom the entrance had been opened? Very soon I had proof that they were not sure the major had told the truth. Ballard walked over to check the mouth of the stream. He didn't like it. He took the cold-water treatment like a man, but he was going no farther. That hole, once you were beyond the entrance, was a fitting home for the nastier spirits of the underworld. He was perfectly right to be content with shining a light inside. At the corner was waiting the were-wolf, but it lay flat behind a boulder and had no intention of appearing till stepped on.

Ballard returned to his fellows and I to the mouth of the channel. For a moment there was such a silence that the faint ripple of the stream seemed to echo back from the walls of their cathedral. Then the dark tunnel of the approach road was faintly illuminated, and the congregation lined itself up, three on one side of the altar and three on the other.

Evans made his dramatic entry in Marrin's blue robe but without his dignity. He was leading the major by a light chain looped around his neck. Denzil seemed submissive, as if he were an animal destined for sacrifice, though whether because he was busy accepting martyrdom or whether any tug on the chain was painful I could not tell. Having arrived in front of the altar, Evans placed him at the center of the circle, lifted off the chain and substituted a wreath of yew. I never admired Denzil more. He took this sinister mummery as impassively as a recruit accepting a slight adjustment of the helmet. His eyes looked proudly into a past known only to him.

On each side of Evans and the major was a line of three holding their torches so that the whole scene was enveloped in a thin red mist. All eyes were on Evans and the altar. Though one line faced me I thought I could take a risk in the prayerful concentration of hocus-pocus. I slipped out into the bed of the stream and crawled down it, hidden by the edge of the cavern floor, until I reached the lake. It was quite shallow where it met the rock and I continued crawling, very gently without making any wash, up to a point where I was below and behind the altar. If Evans went around it or leaned across it he was bound to see me, but so long as he was officiating I was safe.

I had the impression that these raised arms and murmured prayers were a preliminary to something more serious. Preliminary to what? Human sacrifice of course went through my head, but I couldn't believe it. The object of all this was more probably to dedicate the major to the divinity of the altar and so involve him in the mysteries that his religion rather than his body was sacrificed. If so, they underrated their man. They knew that he had a limited sympathy for Broom Lodge faith, though distrusting Marrin and very far from accepting membership. They were also aware that he did not wholly reject — and that's putting it mildly — the conception that the golden cauldron, whether found or materialized by Marrin, could be the Grail. What they did not realize was that he possessed two impregnable fortresses of resistance: that of the trained, sane, devoted Guards officer and a spiritual courage worthy of the Guardian of the Grail.

The prayer meeting broke up. Time passed. Nothing happened. I hugged the sheer bank of the lake below the altar, in deeper shadow now that the torches had moved away. Evans was standing by the windlass erect and silent, his right hand resting on the tail of the dredge, his left Napoleonically thrust into his robe. A group of three were strolling and muttering like monks in a cloister. Two others were away toward the far end of their temple. The seventh was near the junction of stream and lake, and if he had looked to his left he must have seen me or at least a lump where there shouldn't be a lump. Fortunately he walked toward the dark mouth of the stream and stared into it, doubting, I think, if Ballard had done a proper job of exploration.

Still nothing happened. The absence of tension was itself nerve-racking because one dreaded what the climax of the service would be when it was resumed. They might be waiting for midnight or some other propitious hour or possibly for some sign from the major himself. I was again reminded of Mithraic ritual. In that case Denzil was being subjected to the Trial of Fortitude. Would he break down and scream because nobody was paying any attention to him? Would he rush out of the circle and attack the nearest officiant? He stood quite still within the spiritual wall. To the believers the apparent hypnotism may have been impressive magic, but in fact there was no magic about it. Denzil could gain nothing by moving. Escape, one against seven, was impossible. Meanwhile, among the unbounded number of places where he might choose to stand, the circle was the most obvious and most dignified.

Time went on and on until I found that my own fortitude was being severely tested. To lie, cold and motionless as a corpse in the black lake, to do nothing, absolutely nothing, while waiting to observe blood sacrifice or physical torture or the madness of hallucination was torment, and I doubt if I would have had the patience if I had not appreciated that all this seemingly casual idleness was a most effective technique, not only for softening up the victim but for provoking the observer — if there was one — into giving his presence away.

I heard a sort of collective gasp and put my head over the edge. Into the scattered lights of the cavern something advanced down the path. Above it was the shape of the cauldron picked out by red reflections and seeming to be sailing at head height down the tunnel by itself. Every one of the coven was motionless, turned toward it. The major made his first movement. He knelt down. With the slow march of a priestess Elsa in her black robe, the cauldron held with both white arms above her head, walked toward the altar. She was as beautiful and timeless as some worshipper from the walls of an Egyptian tomb bringing an offering to Isis.

If their astonishment had not been so manifest I would have thought they had been waiting for her. Better theory: she was returning the bowl in the hope that if they were holding us they would release us. Impulsive, crazy rescue. Could end disastrously on that altar. What an unparalleled sacrifice of the beauty of the world! All this went through my mind in a second, followed by a savage inspiration direct from Gwyn ap Nudd himself, or at least worthy of him. Evans had backed against the windlass, one robed arm gripping the structure. I crawled quickly behind him, reached up and released the brake.

What I intended — and I swear that was all — was that the handle of the winch should knock him into the water and give us a chance to escape in the confusion. The lower rope came in while the upper rope attached to the heavy dredge whooshed out across the lake. Evans went with it, the flared sleeve of his robe caught in the dredge and possibly his arm as well. He kicked and yelled but there he hung until he splashed into the black mirror and disappeared into that grinning opening between rock and water where the lake continued on to the unknown.

I kept low. Nobody had seen me. Two of them threw off their robes and swam out. A third man ran for the windlass and struggled with the looping rope and the brake. After that he was fully occupied, for I had reached out for the torch he had dropped and set his nightdress on fire.

I yelled to Elsa to run, for she was nearest to the passage. That brought our dreaming Perceval to life. He launched himself from his knees with the dash of the cavalry, butted Raeburn in the wind, doubled him up and raced on to cover Elsa's retreat. Only two of the congregation who had been helplesssly watching the swimmers were ready for action. By the time I had jumped up to dry land and was running for the passage they were almost on me but slowed down by their robes and their torches.

Elsa and Denzil were struggling along in the dark until I was near enough for the beam of my flashlight to show them the way. Together we splashed through the pool and around the buttress of rock, so that our pursuers were momentarily out of sight but far too close for comfort. It occurred to me that when the three of us were scrambling out through the entrance, necessarily in single file, the last one would be caught. So I handed my light to the major and snapped at him to get clear with Elsa and the cauldron, for I knew the way and would be in no danger.

There could be no question of defending the passage without a weapon; they could deal with me by shoving a torch in my face. But what gave me confidence was the patchy light of those torches, showering red smoke and sparks as they ran and illuminating the roof and sides of the gallery without throwing any beam ahead. I let them come around the buttress before I shot off, so giving Elsa and Denzil a good start of some seconds. As I expected, escape was not too difficult. They could see nothing twenty yards ahead of them while I was in a pink, faint dusk just sufficient to prevent me from tripping over any obstacle.

But my brilliant idea turned out disastrously. As I swung around into the straight lateral gallery I saw Denzil's light vanish around the bend far ahead of me — too far ahead of me. The pair had gone straight on, passing Marrin's entrance, and had turned into the blocked shaft. I should have foreseen that could happen. The major, unconscious when he was brought in, had no picture at all of his whereabouts, and Elsa in her rash, passionate attempt to get through and deliver up the cauldron had never glanced back to see what the entrance looked like from below.

The temptation was to follow my love whatever happened; it was too late to shout to them to turn back. Common sense somehow overcame emotion. If I could get out and summon help, it would not be long before the pair of them were free. So I turned right and plunged at the correct entrance with one of my followers so close behind me, owing to my momentary hesitation, that I felt him grab at my ankle as I crawled through. Once clear of the pit props I sprinted and dropped into cover. No nonsense of bonking my pursuer on the head. I had done too much damage already for an explanation in court.

It was the converted boxer who emerged. He relit his torch and had a look around above and below the slope but never spotted me among the tussocky grass. Only when he had returned below did I realize they would assume that all three of us had escaped, not just the mysterious unknown who had released the brakes and set fire to surplices. With sight limited by the wavering red circle of the torches they could not possibly have judged how far ahead was Denzil's light when it disappeared, if indeed they had noticed it at all.

That encouraged me to attempt some immediate tactical surprise rather than to wander off to scattered cottages and try to raise a posse among unbelieving villagers. Provided that I could return unseen and provided that it was at all possible to get a picture of the movements and intentions of these scurrying and disorganized moles I ought to be able to create a diversion. So I returned, wiggling like a snake into its hole and praying that no sound of displaced stone or pit prop would give the movement away.

By this time I was very familiar with the plan of the galleries. It was simple — much like the letter F with a tail. The small bar was the druidicals' entrance and the long bar the original adit, now blocked, where Elsa and the major would be silently crouching and wondering what the devil had happened. At the bottom of the F the gallery curved away downhill until it ended at the pool. I waited at the junction of the small bar and the stem of the F and soon heard the low voices of two or perhaps three in the gallery to my right. It was the most awkward place they could have chosen. There was no hope of reaching Elsa and the major till they were moved: I don't know why they had chosen it — certainly to be at hand in case the fugitives started to put back the pit props, possibly to be able to rush out from the dark directly behind anyone who returned as I had done. They had extinguished their torches.

I felt my way along the cut rock wall, around the corner at the tail of the F and down the passage to see if there was any earthly chance of decoying them away. I could of course hear nothing at all from the direction of the cavern and had to take the gamble that they were all occupied with the rescue of Evans. He would not be very deep down and it would not be difficult to cut him free if one of the fools had a knife and if it were only the robe which was caught. But after that would come the business of resuscitation.

I felt oppressed and defenseless in the absolute darkness. What scared me was that a party might come up bearing Evans and that I should be trapped between them and the picket at the entrance. I suppose that imagined fears are often worse than real danger — which God knows I had been in down below and had not time to think about it.

Halfway down the gallery my misgivings were justified. I heard splashings as feet passed through the pool. The only possible hiding place was the major's home away from home and I slipped inside the recess till the footsteps of one man had safely passed.

When all was quiet I struck matches and ventured a quick look around. It was the changing room. The major and I had seen little sign of it since no solemn ceremony was then going on. There were seven silly little flat cases in which the celebrants had brought their robes. On hangers were three coats and a spare robe. Two spare torches were leaning against the wall beneath them. The oil lamp had been put out.

Marvelous! That was all I needed for my diversion. It was the robe I had set on fire which at once put it into my head. I smashed the lamp and laid one of the torches by its side. On that foundation I built a bonfire of the cases, the robe and the coats, lit the second torch and threw it on.

Smoke poured out of the recess and up the gallery toward the entrance. I hoped that would happen, for it would bring down the alarmed picket at the top while leaving the air of the cavern clear for the present; but I had not reckoned on such a volume of fog in a confined space. We should all have been asphyxiated if my old friend Nodens had not overruled his son and sent flame from heaven to lessen the smoke.

The party from the top came rushing down and entered the cavity coughing and choking. I was outside it, a little distance from the gallery and safe from detection. Holding my wet shirt over my face, I tiptoed past the changing room and ran for the entrance, which seemed to be acting as a chimney. When I had passed it there was little more than haze — for which I thanked God since I had a vision of Elsa and Denzil trapped in their dead end.

I called to them to run toward me and to hold their breath as they dragged themselves out to the open air. Elsa went first while I held the golden cauldron. The major was more alarmed for that than for her, so I handed it over to him and told him to hurry. When I myself reached the surface I had a longish bout of coughing and spitting before I could speak at all. I could only touch Elsa's hand before I threw myself at the job of replacing the pit props.

"We must not close them up," the major protested.

"My God, we must! How do you think that Elsa can face any of them and what lies they are going to tell the commune? Leave them here for a day or two while we think!"

Elsa helped me. The major decided to let Arthurian chivalry go to hell and lent an efficient hand. The Grail, which had escaped with only a slight dent below the rim, sat on the grass and watched us.

"But how?" I asked her.

"Well, I knew they wanted that bloody bowl more than anything else, so when you didn't turn up I thought I'd swap it for you, and for Denzil of course. You had described the place so exactly for me. I got lost all the same and was nearly going to give up when I saw the Broom Lodge van standing on the track. Then I found the old gate to the workings and followed the foot of the slope till I saw the hole wide open."

"But light?"

"Piers, darling, I *am* grown up! I brought a flashlight and then chucked it away as soon as I could see down into the cavern. I thought it would spoil my entry if I didn't use both hands to carry the bowl. Scene Three. Priestess rescues lover. Tripy plot by Verdi and music by Stravinsky."

She began to sob with relief and I held her close.

"What do we do now?" she cried. "I can't go back to Broom Lodge, and you're icy and shivering."

"Stick your robe on him!" the major ordered. "And you can have my parka."

The dark-green parka and her brown tights suited her very well. She reminded me of the Principal Boy in a pantomime. I did not say so. I was so glad that she belonged again to our sanctuary of the trees, not to the altar of black waters. As for me, I tied my wet clothes up in a bundle and put on that fragrant robe. The warmth of her body and laughter when the shoulder seams split, restored me.

"Where are we to go?" she asked. "No hotel would take us."

I said that I could offer some Robin Hood hospitality for the night and that next day we would go to London. Meanwhile she should return to Broom Lodge, pack a case of necessaries and her smartest summer frock and slip out again on foot without being noticed.

She had boldly parked her car — snatched from the communal garage — on the track used by the "geologists" and drove us to the village of Wigpool where I picked up mine. We then made for Broom Lodge, she to the garage and her room, and I to the quiet forest road where I waited for her return.

"Going to the British Museum, Piers?" the major asked.

"Yes, just as we intended before the burglary."

"May I come with you?"

"Of course. Whatever Elsa's bowl is, you are its guardian for the present."

He did not object to my calling it Elsa's bowl. Since strictly speaking, it belonged to the commune, I thought he might and so added the bit about the guardian.

"I have not been found worthy," he said. "She has."

I wasn't going to tell him how the Grail had come into her possession and I doubt if he wanted any prosaic explanation of the mystery. For him it may have been the eternal destiny, or a reward for her selfless gallantry.

Elsa returned out of the night, transformed from priestess via Principal Boy to neatly dressed tourist, hair now primly plaited and coiled. I drove to the glade beneath my gloomy hill where sometimes I left my car and led them up to the den.

"So this is the hotel where you lived!" she exclaimed.

"It is as it should be," the major said, reverently laying down the cauldron on the stump I used as a table. "The vision of the angels and the forest hut."

He must have been referring to one of the Grail legends in which the seeker was led to a humble hut full of light and music. Presumably it was also full of heavenly warmth which my den was not. As the smoke could not be seen by night I lit a fire in the ruined hearth and when I had changed to the gents' suiting of Personality No. 1 we sat around the blaze till the sky behind the line of the Cotswolds, far away across the Severn and its meadows, showed the gray of dawn. My own forest angel slept with her head on my lap.

I put out the fire and rolled the major's blessed car rug around the cauldron, tying it up safely. Dawn and the presence of Elsa and Denzil, one representing the joyous spirit of earth and the other the mysteries of the wandering soul, brought on a moment of adoration. Suppose, I said to myself, I really have got, here rolled up in a rug, the Grail itself or that paragon of beauty which created the myth.

We drove into Gloucester and took the first train up to town. I expected the major to stay at my flat. I had only two bedrooms but there was no need for embarrassment; by this time he knew very well what were the relations between Elsa and myself. He surprised me by saying that he would go to his club; a clothes brush was all he needed, and the valet would supply everything else. Clubs and valets seemed utterly out of character. But why should they? No doubt he wasn't the only eccentric retired officer who turned up fresh from a religious meeting in some obscure and holy Himalayan village or a study of voodoo in the groves of Haiti with nothing but an expensive suit of indestructible tweed.

"No connections half as good as yours, old boy!" he said, "but if Tony is there for lunch I could mention the Museum to him."

I asked who Tony was.

"Sir Anthony Aslington. On some board or other which runs the place."

Aslington was only a name of power to me. There was hardly a national museum of art or antiquities in which he was not chairman of some committee. The best authority I could reach myself was the curator of the Middle Eastern Department.

"And meanwhile you'd better take care of the bowl. Can't allow it to be unpacked by anyone. Can't leave it with the porter."

It was curious how the Guardian could become outwardly the ex-officer of the House Guards. With no apparent stress he left behind the lanced and unstirruped cavalry of Arthur and returned to a world in which the plumes and armor of everyday were real.

"You do the talking when we get to the Museum," he added. "Never was any good at lies!"

Once at home, I managed to make an appointment with my friend, the curator, for next day. Later he telephoned me to change the time as Sir Anthony wanted to be present. What the hell had I got hold of, he asked, that could interest that old sinner? I replied that I didn't know what I'd got but hoped that one of them could tell me, and left it at that.

Elsa refused to accompany us. To be in my flat opened up for her a present and a future for which as abbess she must have longed, and she was bubbling with mischief and gaiety.

"I'd be a distraction," she insisted. "You know what they'd be curious about instead of attending to the bowl. What a pretty piece! You should ask her out to lunch, Tony. Who does she belong to, Colet or Matravers-Drummond? And what would they think of you if it came out that you'd raped me?"

There was only one answer to that piece of impertinence.

I set out next morning with the cauldron in an old-fashioned leather case used for packing top hats and a feeling that I might be walking into trouble. The police had been informed that among the objects stolen from Broom Lodge was a gold bowl. The description of it had been very imprecise, but jewelers and bullion brokers might have been advised to look out for something of the sort. It seemed possible, though very unlikely, that the British Museum had also been warned. I was happier when I called for the major at his club. He had bought a new shirt and tie and looked a personage above suspicion who might easily be Lord Lieutenant of his county but could never have been a burglar, even amateur.

We took a taxi to the Museum and were ushered in to the curator's office. I was impressed by Sir Anthony. He struck me as an authority on art rather than archaeology, which may have been due to his neat, pointed, seventeenth-century beard and the jeweler's loupe slung from a broad black ribbon around his neck. So much the better. The bowl had authorities of two different disciplines to pronounce on it.

Up to a point I came clean. I said that Major Matravers-Drummond in the course of his investigations into esoteric religions had become involved with a strange character who claimed to have rediscovered the secrets of alchemy and had shown him the golden bowl as proof. The major pretended to believe that this character had made it and managed to obtain the loan of it for a day. He had appealed to me for an opinion as I was the only expert at hand, not

realizing that I was a historian of ancient economies and no archaeologist.

Polite chorus of: "No, no. You are well known, Colet. Admirable work in your own field."

Well, I had ruled out transmutation of metals, I said, and when I
had seen the bowl or cauldron I thought it more likely that the
self-styled alchemist was trying to fake an antiquity. I had also
wondered whether it might not be a genuine treasure from some
undeclared discovery of a chieftain's hoard or tomb.

I then took the lid off the hat box and placed my beauty upon
the table. They were both fascinated by it, but the curator ruled
out my buried hoard immediately.

"The gold is thin and unless very solidly protected from falling
material it would have been squashed flat or at least dented by
earth or pebbles. But there is only one small dent below the rim
that looks recent. My dear Piers, it resembles nothing I have ever
seen — Scythian, Scandinavian, Persian, Egyptian. I don't care for
the handles, and my personal opinion is that two years old is more
likely than two thousand."

Sir Anthony praised to the skies the craftsman who had made it,
but added that as an antiquity it would not take in a — he was
about to say "child" but substituted "competent archaeologist."

"We must ask ourselves first what it was for," he went on. "A
cooking pot? Well, you wouldn't dare put it on a hot fire. A mixing
vessel? But that would be a bowl without neck or rim. A Burial
Urn? Wrong shape. The vessel depends for its astonishing beauty
on its form. No decoration at all, which is exceptional. A bedrid-
den emperor's urinal. That's the best I can suggest. And what's
your opinion, Denzil? You sit there saying nothing and looking
guilty. How about that second sight of yours?"

"I can only tell you that in some way it is not of our world at
all," the major said.

"Made at the full moon by a cabalist, eh? But there is something
odd about the glorious color" — he fixed the loupe in his eye and
carried the cauldron to the window — "I have my suspicions. May
I send it down to the lab, Denzil? You can trust them. They won't

need filings. And meanwhile let's have a small decanter of the Museum manzanilla."

The verdict did not take long to come back — the time for two leisurely glasses of sherry and some learned conversation on the techniques of Cretan and Mycenaean goldsmiths to which I contributed little and the major nothing — beyond saying that his alchemist friend was a recluse, worked to his own taste and didn't know whom he was imitating if he was.

The bowl was brought back and a note handed to Sir Anthony.

"As I suspected might be the case," he pronounced, "your cauldron or amphora is of pure gold. Twenty-four carats. Pure. No ancient craftsman would ever have worked in pure gold without any alloy. It's too malleable for any practical purpose. With strong arms you could squash this vessel fairly flat between your palms. Offhand I can think of only one explanation. Your alchemist was hoarding gold as a speculation. He possibly got hold of it illegally. So, being as we all agree a fine goldsmith, he decided to keep it in the form of this vessel rather than in ingots of which the origin could be traced."

That was running close to my early conjecture before I decided on the burial hoard. I said that it seemed an expensive hobby.

The curator, who was probably worried by the rising cost of insuring and guarding his own collection of Near Eastern gold, and kept a close eye on the value of priceless objects if stolen and melted down, at once replied to that.

"It only cost him his time. Weight of your bowl is about 180 ounces. At the beginning of the year the gold price was £600 an ounce. So we can say its value was £108,000. I don't know whether the rarity of pure gold would make it more or less. Gold price now is £670 an ounce. Value of bowl, something over £120,000. Profit just by sitting still for six months, £12,000."

Then Marrin's profit on gold, so long as the price continued to rise, would alone account for the prosperity of his commune without any need for the pretense of alchemy. But what started him off when Broom Lodge was bust and he rescued it? He had not the capital to speculate in gold; and even if he could somehow raise enough to buy, perhaps on margin, what would have happened to his precious commune if the price fell?

No, somewhere there was still a mystery. Marrin had suddenly changed from futile and contemplative salmon fishing to working in gold. That, as Elsa had said, brought prosperity. What then was the object in impressing his public by a skeleton glyptodont and a vessel reputed sacred by the inner circle? Answer, as Sir Anthony had acutely observed: to hide the source of the gold. Was it fraud in South Africa or a dig in Severn meadows or dredging the Wigpool lake or some method of transmutation more scientific than alchemy? We were free to choose which impossibility was the least impossible.

At the Museum there was nothing more to be said beyond our expressions of respect and gratitude. The cauldron was restored to its hatbox — with even more care than before — and we went back to the major's club for lunch. In the taxi we laid off the whole subject except once when I exploded:

"So bang goes your Grail and my Nodens treasure! You do agree, Denzil?"

"With reservations, yes."

"You said once that the Grail could be remade."

"I said the druidicals thought so."

"But you accepted it."

"Pure gold. Inspiration. Wasn't wrong in a way. Give it a rest till after lunch, old boy!"

He was right. The club dining room was no place for discussion of subtleties apart from those of the wine list. And we needed to be fortified against so much disappointment. Afterward, in a quiet, cool corner with brandy in front of us, he said:

"Going on with the search, Piers?"

"Is it worth it?"

"Very strong position you're in. You're just a friend of Simeon who stayed at the commune and came to the funeral. They don't know the wolf's den, don't know he has been watching, don't know who did the damage at Wigpool."

"So what?"

"Got to let 'em loose, haven't we? Badly want the bowl, and can be sure that Elsa has it."

"She's safe with me, and they don't know about us. You didn't."

"Maybe. But wiser to give it up. Police and lawyers likely to be a nuisance too. I'd find another dowry for that splendid girl if I were you. Where did Simeon get his gold?"

"But I haven't a clue."

"Severn, old boy. Bright water and the shadow."

*PART*

Again I must write an exact account of my operations while memory is fresh, in case I am ever compelled to justify them. I feel that I am guilty of a betrayal, yet must admit that the offense lies on me as lightly as do the deaths of Marrin and Evans. I intended neither, but perhaps did not care as much as I should have if my actions were to bring about a highly probable result. A sentence of one year for Marrin would, I think, be ample. My intervention was only culpable negligence. In the case of Evans I could plead self-defense unless witnesses agreed with each other in some outrageous lie, which, thanks to Denzil's mission to the heathen, is now unlikely.

On the whole I see the betrayal of my professional standards as worse than dubious manslaughter. On the other hand I am convinced that it is pointless to publish a discovery which in the absence of date and identity adds nothing material to history.

I return to my confession. The fact that I have just written "confession" shows that my conscience is still uneasy, but to hell with it! If I published I should undoubtedly lose my reputation rather than advance it, and at the same time be forced to throw more light than is convenient on matters which could still, I fear, be of interest to the police.

After the indisputable verdict of Authority on the golden cauldron I repacked it and consigned it to the safe deposit at my bank. The next urgent duties were to recover the major's car before it was found and reported, and to release the prisoners at Wigpool. Meanwhile I left Elsa at my flat, where it was best she should remain until we had dealt with the parishioners of Gwyn ap Nudd and concocted some story to account for her sudden disappearance from Broom Lodge.

In the evening the major and I drove down to the Forest and after dark found his old Humber undisturbed and extracted it from the thicket where it had been hidden. I was growing weary of darkness and straining eyes along the beam of a torch, and wished I had been gifted with night sight: a werecat rather than a werewolf. When we were out in the open we mended the wire, leaving the fence in better condition than before. As soon as the wheel tracks had become barely distinguishable under the growing grass the farmer to whom the derelict copse belonged would never notice that the wire had been cut and repaired.

No lodging was more discreet than the den, so there we remained till morning. I noticed that the major slept where he dropped as easily as any old soldier. That accounted for his patience underground as champion of the imagined Grail. He was divisible by three: one part the wandering friar, one part clubman, one part veteran of the Queen's — or Arthur's — bodyguard.

We were in no hurry to release the druidicals. They had now been buried for three nights and two days, and they could well endure another without food. Excellent fresh water they had in plenty. Before we unearthed them we had to know what their saner companions were doing or had done at Broom Lodge, so in the morning the major, as friend of Simeon Marrin and always welcome visitor, drove over to the commune for the casual call.

He came back with rations and the news. Evans and six others were missing. Elsa was missing too. The colonists assumed she was with the others but were puzzled since they knew that she had mild contempt for the inner circle. Had the police been informed? Well no, they hadn't. General opinion was that the disappearance must be connected with some ritualistic observance. Three days of fasting under the oaks, perhaps. Broom Lodge was of course aware that the adepts did have their places of worship but out of reverence for the mysteries of others — inspired by Marrin himself rather than the characters of his disciples — refrained from tasteless curiosity. Another good reason for not reporting the missing persons was that the commune disliked the police on principle. Working for the future and happy in the present they felt no need for the protection of law.

All the commune knew of Wigpool was that Marrin had done some casual search for ores which he needed in the laboratory. Another tour of nearby pubs confirmed that Broom Lodge need never come into the picture at all. Marrin, with his genius for staging a convincing scenario, had set a story going that assays of minerals were occasionally carried out for the training of students in geology. That accounted for the tracks of vehicles and signs of excavation.

In the last of the twilight and an empty countryside we came upon the Broom Lodge van still standing at the end of the rough lane. It was safe enough there and the odd villagers who might have passed it would naturally assume that the "geologists" were at work nearby or perhaps camping for a night or two. We approached the low heap of pit props silently, and listened. Nothing to be heard. Then we tried the blocked gate to the old workings. There they had been at desperate work, for a hole had been scraped out of the timbers which ended at the iron bars above and below the slit. It appeared to have been done laboriously with a knife, and all the chap had gained by a blistered palm was the certain knowledge that the bars were too close together for a body to pass through. There, too, we could not hear a sound, but that meant little. The loudest speech could not carry around two corners of the gallery.

We started very cautiously to remove the pit props until only four were left, quite easy to push aside. Obviously the condemned were so demoralized in the darkness that they had given up hope and possibly were huddled together in the changing room which might retain some warmth from my bonfire. We wanted them out and away, so I went down as far as the cross gallery thudding on the floor with a pit prop and hammering against the rock wall. At last I heard somebody feeling his way up, falling and, instead of cursing, sobbing at his helplessness. I came up, cleared the hole completely and we settled down in a dry ditch close to the van to await their arrival.

It took the best part of an hour. Perhaps some of them had to be fetched up from the great cavern — a difficult journey through black nothing, even though the way could not be missed. Torches would have burned out long since and the batteries of flashlights gone flat. They must have had some in order to get from the entrance to the changing room; now that I think of my fast and spontaneous activities, I believe there was a pocket flashlight in each of the coats I threw on the flames.

They whimpered with relief when they found their truck still in its place and collapsed against it, their dim figures looking like life-size rubber dolls simultaneously deflating. There were only six of them, and they were in no state to go hunting in the dark for the persons who had set them free. Somebody said:

"Could you finish the windlass?"

"Not the lot. Couldn't in the dark. Most of it has gone."

A voice I recognized as Ballard's whined:

"The wind! Oh, the wind!"

There was not much of it. A damp, cool breeze. But when, as I myself had found, one has been wet, hungry and cold for so long fresh air is altogether too fresh.

"Who let us loose?"

"Same man who shut us in."

"I've told you. It was Elsa."

They could have no doubt that Elsa had acquired the bowl exactly as and when she did, but I gathered there had been a disagreement on whether she had made her dramatic appearance in order to save the major and/or the unknown, or whether she had boldly attempted to take over her uncle's high priesthood to which Evans had succeeded.

Apparently that was not unthinkable. As opposed to some of their eastern doctrines, they allowed women to have souls. I should bloody well hope so! I know men who are so single-minded that the chance of eternal life for them will be a case of win or lose. But women have as many aspects as a diamond and at least one facet must be immortal if anything is.

They must have debated the question of Elsa over and over again as well as the mystery of the major's companion. That they touched on just enough to confirm my opinion that I had not been identified, and slopped themselves into the van. To judge by the driver's course down the track I could only hope that the hour was too late for much traffic on the forest roads and that none of what there was would have the bad luck to meet him.

"Poor sods! Only misguided!" the major exclaimed with a pity I had not expected. "They are not likely to return. But we will now go down and deliver them from further temptation."

I said that we should need explosives to close the place for good.

"Didn't mean the way of the body, Piers. Way of the soul what matters."

I was in no mood for any of his theological hairsplittings but there was another good reason to go back: to see that Evans's body had not been left about. Abruptly and as never before I was shocked to realize how the innocent and happy colonists were involved in criminality without being aware of it. Inner circle was a misnomer. A better picture of Broom Lodge was a figure eight with a small loop at the top and a larger one at the bottom and the fraudulent but impressive magus at the junction.

When we reached the great cavern it was plain that the work of dismantling the windlass and removing all traces of occupation had been interrupted by lack of light. The main wheel, weighed down by axle and fittings, had been sunk in the lake. Most of the superstructure remained, but bolts and lashings had been partly loosened so that it was easy to demolish the lot and to steer the floating timbers and ropes to the other side of the cavern where the current of the stream slowly carried them away to oblivion under the low roof.

There was no sign of the exact fate of Evans. The swimmers must have been able to disentangle him from the dredge, but when they found that he had been under too long to be revived I suppose they pushed the body out as far as they could and weighted it. Their anxiety to leave no trace of recent occupation seemed to me exaggerated. The cavern and its lake might, however, be rediscovered at any time — since rumor proved that it had been visited in the past — and they wanted no awkward questions. Nor, for that matter, did I.

The major now turned to delivering them from temptation. With the energy of a Round Table champion he attacked the altar of the pagans with a heavy balk of timber. I helped him with some regret. The altar, and especially the pedestal for the cauldron, had its own beauty like everything Marrin touched. Fortunately he thought more of proportions than good mortar, or else it had not set properly in the prevailing damp. Splash after splash his cut ashlars were drowned in the lake.

Returning to the surface, we bedded down the pit props and scattered loose ones above them, re-creating the illusion of a derelict pile which had been there for years. While we were driving home to the den I asked the major what story he thought the six would tell when they arrived at Broom Lodge. He was far more conversant with the social diversities of the commune than I was.

"Anything. Any mystery," he replied. "The rest of the colony won't care where they have been."

"But what about Evans?"

"After long prayer and meditation he left them to seek further enlightenment."

"The commune will let them get away with that?"

"No reason to disbelieve. And thankful to be rid of him."

"Who will take over?"

"Democracy, old boy."

"But democracy needs a chairman."

"He'll appear. Pity to see the place all sixes and sevens. I used to enjoy it. Simeon and all. Guest room always ready. So I think I'll go back for a bit."

"What on earth for?"

"Boring from within, Piers. Boring from within."

I insisted that it was dangerous and that he shouldn't take the risk.

"No risk. If I'm dead, I can't let on where Elsa and the bowl are. They know I know. But if I say nothing about Wigpool, all they can say is: 'Good morning, major. Nice day!' Easy to keep 'em in order while they're off balance."

"And Elsa? What will you tell the commune about her?"

"That she couldn't stick working with Evans and cleared out in a temper. Might come back when she hears that Evans has gone."

"How could you know?"

"Ran into her in Gloucester, Piers. She was seeing Simeon's lawyer to sign some papers."

I remarked too lightly that for someone who disapproved of lying, that was a beauty. He took it almost as an insult, informing me as if I were a junior fellow officer that to preserve the honor and safety of a woman a lie was not only permissible but a duty. He was still in a mood for military snorts until we were back in the den and had opened a bottle.

We could not sleep. The little pool of lamplight in the clearing, surrounded by the wall of larches seeming as black and solid as the impenetrable rock, was a continuance of our ordeal.

"I think you want to give back the cauldron," I said at last.

"Yes — on conditions. Summon the bright water for your girl's dowry!"

"It's never bright. A dirty blue under the sun. Milk chocolate under cloud."

"Let's walk to the top of your hill, Piers."

We pushed our way up to the peak, where through the slender trunks we could watch the great expanse of the Severn Sea silently sliding down to the ocean at half tide and under a half-moon.

"Gold under the silver, Piers. You've forgotten it in all this sordid excitement."

In the morning I again tried to stop him from setting out upon his new illusion of himself as missionary to the pagans or whatever he meant by "boring from within." It was no use. The only indication he gave of any lack of confidence was to tell me — should I not be far away and not wish to appear in person — to look for any message at our old ash stump and leave a reply.

When he had gone I cleared up the den since it was unlikely that the wolf would need it anymore. Meanwhile my thoughts played for the hundredth time over the dreams and contradictions in the major's character. The Gloucester solicitor, who had caused the temporary coldness between us, kept recurring to mind. He really existed and was Marrin's unfortunate executor. I had his name and address from Elsa, who was about the only person able to answer questions on the assets of the commune though she couldn't make much sense of them. I decided on the spur of the moment to call on this Mr. Dunwiddy as a friend and guest of Broom Lodge. He might refuse to talk to me as having no standing in Marrin's affairs but, if he did talk, some clue to the source of Marrin's capital might come out of it.

Dunwiddy's office was in the cathedral close. I think I would rather live in such a place than anywhere else in England. All the benediction of the land is there from the devotion of the Norman architects struggling with traditions of Byzantium to the ecstasies in stone of the fifteenth century and around the lawns shapely Georgian houses of the servants of the great church. I am overcome by the sanity of it all rather than by any religion, mindful that before this Christian civilization there were few peaceful havens for the soul. It was no place for an executor of Simeon Marrin who served past and future gods by blood on a torch-lit altar or slower death in the quicksand of Box Hole.

Dunwiddy was a round ball of a man with a fitting rotundity of wit and wisdom. He made me wait some time, but as soon as he had opened his office door and set eyes on me, received me with a cordiality for which I could not account.

He led me to talk of my interest in ancient economies and thus, via agriculture in the Forest of Dean, eased the way to my impressions of Broom Lodge.

"I trust, Mr. Colet, that the commune will now farm the her-editament with enterprise and without enthusiasm."

Catching his obscure meaning, I replied that I did not think belief in reincarnation ever had much effect on their efforts to make the place pay.

"Indeed, I myself do not order my day to conform with the cathedral chimes, except that I go home at compline when they, I understand, exchange the plow for meditation and the ministrations of the admirable Elsa. By the way can you tell me where she is?"

"I don't know. I understand she left very suddenly."

"Come, come, Mr. Colet! There was a day when local business compelled me to take luncheon in Thornbury. It so happened that I saw Adam and Eve — fully clothed, I assure you — walking in the garden. I am old but not old-fashioned. And as an experienced solicitor I recognize a distinction between love in the eyes and eying with love. I hope that for your sake and hers you are only observing a gentlemanly discretion when you tell me that you do not know where she is."

I allowed him to think so and said that in fact she had gone to stay with my mother.

"Excellent! Excellent! Would you be good enough to let her know that I am anxious to see her?"

"Of course. Can I help at all?"

"I doubt it. No one ever can. It is a question of a car which presumably should be included in Mr. Marrin's estate. The boat which contributed to his sad end is obviously the property of the commune, though an unpleasant, puritan sort of fellow named Evans with whom I had a preliminary talk knew nothing about it. The car, now. A good lady at Bullo is sure that he sometimes crossed the river at night and returned before dawn. The police have made inquiries whether anything was known — let us say of a secret liaison — at Overton or Arlingham. Nothing. And you will agree, Mr. Colet, that in small villages scandal, often amounting to criminal slander, is the breath of life. So the police were sure that Mr. Marrin's business was further afield and that he must have had a car at his disposal. They found it. He kept it in an outlying barn which he had rented at Fretherne — a remarkably quiet hamlet just above Hock Cliff. It was a gray Morris, as inconspicuous at night as a gray rabbit. So, it appears, was he. It's quite extraordinary how so commanding, unforgettable a man could drift out of Broom Lodge leaving no more trace behind him than a ghost — in the existence of which, as he once informed me when I was engaged on a breach of tenancy due to persistent haunting, he firmly believed."

I could not help Mr. Dunwiddy, but he had helped me. I had never thought of a car permanently garaged on the left bank within easy reach of Marrin's landing place. All I knew — and that I kept to myself — was that he set out on a falling tide which would carry him over the river to the Hock Cliff. He had then only to wait for the flood to carry him back again to Bullo. What did he do meanwhile?

After I left the solicitor's office I decided to cover again, this time by car, all the left bank of the Severn where I had walked and waded in search of an unknown Roman port. My theory of a treasure — of Nodens, as I had called it — which Marrin had dug up was not demolished at all; only the cauldron was. Without doubt it was modern and he had made it, but of pure gold which, according to the Museum, no craftsman, ancient or modern, would use.

The site must be too far from Hock Cliff to walk. That stood to reason anyway. Before the desolate stretches of seawall were built the river plain on the left bank was flooded at high tide and must have been a network of mud and marsh at low. So the bank itself could be eliminated as fit for a burial mound or temple treasury, as well as the miles of meadow intersected by pills which even today could overflow when a spring tide came up with a southwest wind behind it. Where did he go in that inconspicuous Morris? Between dusk and dawn he had time enough to reach far into the Cotswolds, dig and return.

The devil! In all this line of speculation I had forgotten that Marrin's case with all his diving equipment was in the dinghy. So it had to be the Severn and nowhere else. And he would dive from the bank as he always did, not from an unstable boat. But why not take the boat all the way to the chosen site? Answer simple. If he went down on the tide beyond Hock Cliff and the Noose he would never be nearer to the left bank than mud flats.

I wasted two days on the job, spending the nights at Gloucester. An utterly frustrating period with gray clouds spitting drizzle at me above and Severn mud over my boots below. In the back of the car was all my equipment for diving, but I had no need to unpack it. I ruled out the sandbanks and the shoals which could never be excavated by a single-handed diver. I ruled out the low red cliffs of marl and sandstone constantly eaten away by the torrents of the ebb to form beaches. I ruled out pills and meadows. In all the centuries from the Bronze Age onward no one would ever have buried a chieftain or built a temple where the next spring tide would turn the site to marsh and a year later to a mudbank separating two new channels. So I gave up and returned to London and Elsa.

I had called her up every evening and gathered that she was happy window-shopping, sight-seeing and appreciating a solitary holiday in my flat after the insistent group society of Broom Lodge. I found her more delicious than ever. The abbess had fallen away along with her robes and there she was on the new wings of womanhood, lovely, intelligent, irreverent and spreading around her an infectious delight in being alive.

On the second day when we came home from celebrating our reunion by a lunch far too joyously expensive for a second-rate historian of ancient economies, the telephone was ringing and she jumped to it — for in my experience no woman will ever let an insistent telephone alone — though the call had to be for me. But it wasn't.

"It's the major for me," she said, her hand over the mouthpiece, and carried on a conversation of which I could make little at her end. She too looked puzzled.

"He says that all of them need me, and there's no risk from the half-wits. I'm holy or something."

"That's what he said about himself."

"They are running short of cash, he says, and we should return Uncle Simeon's brooches and ashtrays and things. What does he mean?"

The major had clean forgotten that we had never told Elsa that he was the burglar. Now that had to come out.

She listened to my story disapprovingly.

"But I still don't see why he did it," she said.

"For the sake of his old friend. I should never have agreed but I did. You see, he didn't believe in the alchemy for a moment. He was afraid that your uncle was stealing gold somewhere or that he was faking antiquities to sell them as genuine finds. I suspected — and I still do — that he had really found a buried hoard and was breaking it up. Iniquitous! So we determined to get hold of the cauldron for a couple of days so that I could take it to the British Museum. But Denzil was always halfway to believing it might be the Grail and his nerve failed him. He wouldn't lay hands on it. So he left it and just emptied out the drawer of trinkets. That's what we have to return."

"Denzil Matravers-bloody-Drummond behaved like a two-year-old," she exclaimed, "and you too. And then you have to carry out this crazy plan on the night Uncle Simeon was drowned!"

"We didn't know he was going to be drowned," I said weakly.

"Well, you should have known. And what did you precious pair do with the swag? Of course it must be returned at once."

Not a word about the cauldron, which was just as much the commune's property as the rest.

"It's up at the den."

"Well, we must go down and get it."

We drove down to the Forest which gave her time to recover her — for these days — usual frivolity. She saw the major's professional management of window glass and exit by the drainpipe as pure comedy, and said that in the future the commune should be more careful of its guests and not admit burglars and dissolute snakes in the grass. When we arrived at the den, which she had seen only at night and in the presence of the major, she examined it all with the disparaging interest of a young wife inspecting her husband's bachelor flat and after bouncing provocatively on my former bed of twigs drove me away on the grounds that it was prickly.

The major's bag containing the trinkets was buried under the iron plate which had been my roof. I dug it up and handed it over.

"We can't just walk into Broom Lodge with it," she said.

"That had occurred to me."

"Well, what are you going to do about it?"

"Leave it to Nodens. His specialty is returning lost property."

"I wish you'd stop talking about Nodens as if you believed in him."

"I do — half."

"Well put up a prayer — half."

To amuse her, I did, wondering with too personal and academic humor how I should address him. I didn't know any old Welsh and Nodens certainly didn't know Anglo-Saxon since the invaders never paid any attention to him. So I tried him in Latin.

*Deus piscium siderisque, Nodens immutabile, adesto propitius* — followed by my very reasonable request for a good idea.

Now I swear that it was at that very moment when I was thinking of Nodens on his hilltop commanding the river from the Horseshoe Bend to — to what? — that I was inspired. If the river ended anywhere and became the sea, it was at the Shoots. The underwater gorge at the time of Nodens the God must have been much as it is now: a deep, narrow, navigable channel. But far earlier, in the blossoming years between the retreat of the ice and the return of the sea, the Severn, still a river of fresh water, poured in rapids or perhaps a fast, silver stream through the Shoots and on through the forests which are now the shoals of the Bristol Channel. Why had I not thought of that? Bright water, and the shadows of the gorge.

"And what did Nodens say?" she asked.

"That we should bung the bag in some bushes as if the burglar had dropped it and let the colonists find it."

"I could have told you that without bothering Nodens."

It really only occurred to me afterward that Nodens had answered a quite different question, always assuming that the incorporeal communicates through the imagination: the sole medium we can offer.

At the nearest village I asked Elsa to telephone Denzil to meet us at the sapling stump. I did not wish to visit Broom Lodge or to let my voice be heard so as to ensure the anonymity of the mysterious being responsible for the disasters at Wigpool. Even a glimpse of the way I walked or held my head might remind one of the druidicals of the back view he had seen.

The major was at the rendezvous when we arrived. I could see by his cheerful appearance that the Guards officer was for the time being in total control of the visionary. I asked how the boring from within was going.

"No need to bore, old boy. Damn glad to see me, they were! They miss Simeon. Nobody to give orders. Can't run committees because they all agree with each other. All equal, you see. Too happy to argue. Outsider — that's where I come in. Don't have to be equal. Just occurred to them that half the stuff they make in workshops is unsalable. Training for reincarnation all very well, but got to eat in this life. I've suggested that saddlery would be an improvement on sailmaking."

"Reincarnation backward, Denzil?"

"I have already told you that backward is as likely as forward and perfectly compatible with the faith of a Christian," he pronounced with dignity.

"And the six?"

"Very quiet. I told you they would be. Their gods have let them down. The commune's come around to seeing them as a nuisance. Took it for granted when Simeon was alive that they had the secrets of the universe. Not so sure now."

"And am I holy just to that lot or everybody?" Elsa asked.

"That lot. Priestess of the Grail. All they have left to hang on to."

"Not me! I've had enough as abbess."

"It shouldn't bother you, girl. They'll keep their mouths shut and just give you a nod in passing as they did to your uncle."

"And stare at me. No!"

"Think of the rest of them then! There you were, chief clerk in the orderly room filling up the government forms. All at your fingertips!"

Seeing that her devotion to the commune made her hesitate I told the major that it was out of the question. I needed her. After that she could decide for herself.

Only she and no other person could be allowed to accompany me in what I was proposing for myself. I had given agitated weeks of my life to solving the problem of the gold and it had become an obsession. I had to have a yes or no. Nodens's inspiration might end in a triumph for underwater archaeology or a dowry for Elsa or another body coming up on the tide to Sharpness Docks. That was why I said that later she could decide for herself. The commune could fill a very empty space.

I could see that she thought me somewhat cold-blooded to suggest that she might return to wasting herself in the service of Broom Lodge. She dismissed the subject at once and came to the point of our visit.

"Here's your bag, Denzil! Where will you leave it to be found?"

"Mustn't let the druidicals find it. That would start them up again like the chap who found his watch where Piers put it. Let me see! Burglar goes around house in his car. No reason why he should drop it and run. But he might hide it, intending to come back for it later. We need a new pit for the garbage."

"We do," Elsa agreed. "I've been at them for months to dig it out."

"Good! House Committee will vote on it. Just organized. Got it in my pocket. Dig a new dump and lo and behold there's the bag at a depth of two feet. Ah, yes! And three or four lengths of wire sticking out from it so that if the burglar misses the exact place the first time, he's bound to hit a wire."

"Have you done much burglary, major?" Elsa asked with pretended innocence.

"First offense. Sentenced to community service. Can always take it up again if required. Where are you two off to now?"

"With the permission of the Regatta Committee we are going to inspect the boat at Bullo and see what state it's in." I said.

But before that I had to take a long look at the Shoots and the English Stones, which I had never seen. If we hurried we could get there by road at the bottom of the tide, just as Marrin had done. Had done? That revealed the impatience of my mood. Might just possibly have done would have been a more reasonable thought.

Marrin's motive in trying to drown me because he was afraid I would bring package tours of archaeologists to trespass in his underwater preserves had always seemed inadequate. I had told him of the new interest in riverside caves and shelters where Paleolithic man might have lived before or soon after the Ice Age when water levels were far lower than now. He insisted, rightly, that all the sheer banks of Severn had long since been eaten away to shoals and beaches. I tried to remember whether I had ever mentioned the Shoots. Well, yes, I had. I had said that the only possible site would be the Shoots at the entrance to the Bristol Channel. Since then I had never given that underwater gorge a thought. Of course I hadn't. I had been thinking of man living on fish and game in natural shelters along the river, and I said he would have been as comfortable as any Canadian Indian. But that primitive hunter, Paleolithic or early Neolithic, had not discovered gold and would not be burying chieftains in splendor.

Yet the gorge of hard rock, that deep and narrow channel where the tide could run at ten knots carrying shipping up to and down from the river ports, fitted all requirements. During his salmon days Marrin in his mystic self-confidence might well have tried diving where the fish must pass but neither nets could be used nor weirs built; and then if he had found something other than salmon worth diving for, he could drive down from the barn at Fretherne in an hour, timing his arrival for slack water — diving any other time would be impossible or highly dangerous — and return to

Hock Cliff to catch the flood tide which would take him home to Bullo.

The weather was foul as it could be, the sky gray all over with frequent black clouds driven by a westerly and depositing their rain at the first feel of the land. I was impatient to get away, for there was a full moon and the bottom of the spring tide at the Shoots would be about six P.M. Elsa did not complain. She knew of my obsession with the search but not exactly what I was looking for. I did not know myself.

We ran down to Chepstow with the Severn Bridge in sight most of the way: an unbelievably thin line looking like a tightrope with toy cars balanced on it. Crossing the bridge we turned south down the left bank to Severn Beach, which I had thought must be a playground for Bristol but in fact was an ugly little nineteenth-century village with a small trailer site, tucked in behind a formidable seawall and without a sight of the water.

From the top of the seawall the view was of utter desolation, made still more melancholy by the savage sky. For a mile and a quarter the English Stones extended out into the last of the Severn, forming a flat waste of rock, mud and seaweed indented by scores of ragged, brownish lagoons. The Shoots, separating the English Stones from similar weed-covered rocks on the Welsh side, was barely distinguishable from where we stood — only a lighter streak of water. One longed for the tide to turn and cover the obscene nakedness of a seabed which should never have been revealed.

As the rain lashed this sunless, sorrowful Acheron where once had been forest and meadow before the ocean, higher and higher year after year, stripped it down to the bare, black rock, I could not believe that Marrin had ever walked and waded over it to reach the Shoots with time to dive and return. He must have had a boat to take him all or part of the way to the rock face where he plunged in.

Severn Beach had a pub, and we were both in need of something stronger than the all-pervading water. We went in and shook ourselves. Nobody was in the bar. The campers and local inhabitants must have been waiting for the rain to stop. The landlord, too, seemed to be feeling that he was as isolated as any lighthouse keeper at this shabby frontier of the land.

"Beats me why they come here!" he complained. "No beach. Nothing to do. Can't get a view of anything except the wall. Go up it and you'll get blown off as likely as not. Go down t'other side and up to your ankles in mud."

That gave me an outside chance. In such a place Marrin must have been noticed.

"My brother used to come down here sometimes," I said. "He's in the Ministry of Agriculture and Fisheries and was making a count of conger eels or something. You may remember him. A tall man with a gray Morris car."

"Saw him once or twice I did, but he didn't come in here. Used to turn up toward dusk near the bottom of the tide and row out along the side of the Stones."

"He always was a chap for taking risks."

"Oh, it's safe enough under the shelter of the rocks. But you wouldn't want to be out there when they're covered and a wind like today."

"Where did he hire his boat?"

"None around here. Bought it upriver somewhere, and kept it in the pill up at New Passage."

We drove a mile up the empty road to New Passage, where formerly there was a ferry to the Welsh shore and a pier built out over part of the Stones. The road ended at a gate leading to true Severn country of river meadow and a low seawall. Without arousing any curiosity Marrin could have left his car there like any other tourist out for a riverside walk or a view stretching from the Black Mountains to the Cotswolds. Beyond the remains of the pier was the mouth of a small pill with a rowing boat, high and dry, moored by a long chain. He could never have reached it at half tide, but did not want to. At or near low water it was easy enough to get at it over a beach of shale and mud.

Right! That was all I needed to know except what I should find where the far edge of the English Stones dropped sheer into the Shoots. We would chug downriver from Bullo on the tide and take our time returning on the flood. That was impossible for Marrin if he wanted to do the journey out and back on the same night keeping his movements and his cargo secret.

Next morning we went to inspect Marrin's dinghy, which had been returned to its moorings at Bullo Pill. As it had been picked up in the open sea after spinning away from any soft bank it had touched, the hull was in good condition. Engine and propeller needed some routine maintenance but then started at the second pull. The sun was out, and the west wind had died away to a gentle breeze giving a helpful popple on the water that would show me the course of the channel if in doubt.

There was no reason why we should not make our first attempt on the Shoots that evening, so I filled up the tank and carried on board suit, Aqualung, mask and life jacket. Remembering too vividly the night of Marrin's death, I had to suppress a feeling of repugnance as we left the pill on the same course with the ghost of myself following in the wake.

Swooping under Hock Cliff, around the Noose and over to the right bank we ran down ten miles to Lydney harbor and had lunch. I explained to Elsa more or less what I intended to do. She was a little concerned for me — since that savage sea desert of Stones was too pressing a memory — but I pointed out untruthfully that I was as experienced as her uncle, and anything he could do I could better. Personally I was more alarmed by the startling speed of the ebb tide as those low red banks swept past. Severn shoals were mercifully soft but if I made a mistake we might have to spend the night on one.

It was too late to get out of Lydney into the fairway across the top of Lydney Sand, so I took the channel between the shore and the Shepherdine Sands — where in my opinion the Roman galleys rowed up to their basin — and thanked the lord that the dinghy drew only about eighteen inches. I ran aground once with the Guscar Rocks in sight, but was off again without incident, while Elsa needlessly held her breath, out into the main shipping channel and under Severn Bridge. We were now aiming for the Shoots and if I was carried through I could never get back again before the flood, so I hugged the messy left bank, which would have given a Severn pilot fits, and very cautiously nosed my way along the English Stones until I found a miniature harbor about the size of a bus. It may well have been there that Marrin anchored his rowing boat while he walked out to the Shoots.

I had often wondered why he found it advisable to cross from Bullo to Hock Cliff and then drive the rest of the way downriver instead of taking the road through Chepstow to the Welsh bank and making a crossing of a mere mile to the English Stones. Now I understood it. The Welsh coast was too close. Although he dived, so far as I know, only when slack water fell in the hours of darkness, he risked being seen starting out, returning, mooring. Somebody was sure to be sufficiently curious to follow him and find out what the hell he was doing at the edge of the Shoots. However, if he rowed out from New Passage, utterly deserted, he would be lost against the background of the Stones, sure of the secrecy of his movements and — more important still — of his return with a cargo in the bottom of the boat.

I scrambled out to the west end of the English Stones, and there below me was the last of the ebb sliding as smoothly as a conveyor belt and a lot faster down the deep channel of the Shoots, not more than five hundred yards wide between the Stones and Gruggy Island. Then I went back to the boat to change and out again to a smooth shelf with a clean-cut edge to it. The cliff looked like the gorge wall it was, and I sat there with the water some eight feet below me until the level had dropped another inch or two and all was dead calm. New Passage and Severn Beach were too far away for me to be clearly seen, and I hoped that from the Welsh coast I would appear only a foolhardy trailer owner in a life jacket mucking about on the Stones.

I had told Elsa that I should not be more than twenty minutes underwater and would give her a wave when I was about to dive. When she waved back I plunged in. The silt, no longer carried by the current, was sinking with me like a sparse flurry of yellow snow. Visibility was very poor, but better over the clean rock bottom close under the cliff. I passed a sloping ledge halfway down which could have been a beach and a much wider one nearer the bottom worn by the ice. The face of the rock was cut by vertical fissures and crevices much like the many inlets on the surface of the Stones. I worked southward until I came across a promising cave, which might well have been inhabited in the Stone Age, and explored it at length, my interest now being purely and enthusiastically archaeological without a thought of Marrin and his gold.

I found nothing. When I shot out into the channel I was seized by an invisible, irresistible power and swept northward along the side of the gorge. The tide had turned. Keeping with difficulty close to the cliff I was taken on an underwater tour faster than I could swim and had a salmon's eye view of the rock formations as I was hurried past. I surfaced just in time and found myself swirling around the northern corner of the Stones. From there it was easy enough to swim to our miniature harbor. Elsa was on the rock with her eyes so firmly fixed on the point from which I had dived that she didn't see me until I came alongside her.

On the last sweep past the face of the Stones I had spotted two points of genuine interest. One was just such a shelter as I had described to Marrin. There was a wide stone ledge with the cliff above it deeply undercut marking the bank of the river as it would have been — at a guess — two or three thousand years after the ice had retreated toward Scotland and before the river had become a tidal estuary. To one side of the shelter was a darkness which looked as if it might be a cave. The second interesting discovery was a little deepwater harbor where a boat could lie safely, given a heavy stone or a pinnacle of rock to act as a bollard.

The combination exactly suited Marrin's requirements, but what in God's name he had been diving for I could not imagine. A treasure of gold was no more likely than the nest of a sea serpent preying on mariners. The skills of the riverside family, if there was one, behind their curtain of hides at the entrance to that cave would have been limited to bone fishhooks and tridents with points of flint. Elsa suggested that a Spanish galleon had gone aground on the Stones, but there would be some record of such a spectacular wreck supplying enterprising Gloucestershire fishermen with cash and timber for years to come. My whole hypothesis was ridiculous and archaeologically impossible.

We crossed the river and put up for the night at Beachley almost under the Severn Bridge, intending to return to Bullo, or as near as we could get, on the next day's tide. Elsa telephoned Broom Lodge to let the major know where we were. Some minutes passed before she could get hold of him. Meanwhile the person on the other end, who she thought was Raeburn, far from treating her as holy told her that she must return, almost adding "or else." Denzil too was short and, without mentioning me or our address, said that he would drive over in the morning. It sounded as if he might be having trouble with the pagans.

He turned up after breakfast. It appeared that the six druidicals were spending their nights in the Forest and their days in sleep. They did not work and they did not attend the gentle periods of meditation, separating themselves completely from their once happy companions who were worried about them rather than resentful.

The bag of Marrin's little masterpieces had been found, but the inner circle did not share in the openhearted rejoicings of the community. They never ascribed the return of the lost property to Nodens as I was sure they would. They knew too well that Elsa must have taken the cauldron from the laboratory and assumed that she was responsible for the entire burglary. From their silences and the contemptuous arrogance of their faces the major had the impression that they were not taken in by his explanation that the burglar had buried the bag intending to return for it later, and that they thought it was Elsa who had done it.

"We'll have no peace until the bowl is back," he said.

"Better tell them that it's a modern fake and get a certificate from the Museum."

"It is not a fake, Piers."

"Still the Grail?"

"It can be the Grail recoverable in spirit but not in fact."

"Like Arthur's cavalry?"

"At last you have understood, Piers. Indeed like Arthur's cavalry."

I let it go at that. The major's abstruse heresies were endurable after dinner or in the peace of the Forest, but not soon after breakfast.

He knew nothing of our expedition to the Shoots and I told him the whole futile story.

"It didn't fit your bright water and shadow but long ago it might have done."

"Just daydreams, old boy. Get 'em while I'm shaving sometimes. Mustn't take them too seriously."

"You weren't shaving when you told me the glyptodont was a pet. You had been taking pictures of it for me."

"Pet? Did I say pet? What sort of pet?"

"Don't you remember?"

"Yes, now. Like a rabbit."

"The glyptodont wasn't a bit like a rabbit."

"But edible."

"One doesn't usually eat pets."

"Like a rabbit," he repeated. "Buy it to eat and then become too fond of it."

"My Spanish galleon!" Elsa exclaimed. "Perhaps the ship took on board a live glyptodont in America for the captain's table and by the end of the long voyage he was feeding it from his golden plate."

I said that glyptodonts were extinct long before Columbus, but her phrase "the end of a long voyage" was working in me. Did the glyptodont come from the English Stones? If it did, it must have been brought there by ship.

Long voyage. America too far. Where was that sunken land to the west in which the Welsh bards believed? Atlantis? Well, I've always been damned sure that Atlantis wasn't Santorini. When a colossal eruption overwhelmed it, Mycenaean and Egyptian civilizations were going strong. Yet there is not a word or the vaguest reference to so great a tragedy in Homer or the myths or the hieroglyphs.

Plato's Atlantis is far older. We can date it — so far as one can date a myth — from 9000 to 8000 B.C. A thousand years earlier, as the ice retreated, temperatures had begun to go up and thereafter sea levels were steadily rising about three feet every century, putting the fear of the gods into every settlement by the shore. Geologists can't place the lost low-lying land, yet there must have been a dozen such along the Atlantic coasts which were happy isles until overwhelmed like the green meadows on the English Stones. At least one of them could have preceded Egypt in its civilization, its temples and its harbors.

By God, I can see the fugitives pulling up the long river, too narrow perhaps to use the square lugsail which had brought them in from the ocean, and entering the gorge against the powerful current from the last glaciers on the Welsh mountains, too strong for broken oars and weary arms; but here was a beach for the keel, a platform of rock on which to unload the cargo and stretch their limbs and a cave for shelter. Upstream beyond the gorge they could see the blue river running through open, friendly woodland with deer drinking in the shallows. The voyage was over.

Gold. Can we accept that a high and isolated Stone Age culture, practicing agriculture and possessing seagoing ships, could have discovered gold before any other metal? Easily! Geology alone is enough to account for the absence of tin and copper but plentiful gold. In the empire of the Incas that useful and malleable material had no exaggerated value. The best jugs and bowls were of gold, not of earthernware or bronze (though by then they had discovered it) and the most deadly weapons were still of stone. For how long had such a culture, there or elsewhere, been in existence? There is no evidence. But if you sailed off from such a land into the unknown you would assume that other societies were much like your own and take with you gold for gifts and for trading.

"We shall go back this evening and have another look at slack water," I told the major.

"Useless, old boy! You said so yourself. And bloody danger-ous!"

"I've eaten armadillo and it was quite good."

"You're in one of your dreams. Come off it!" Elsa said.

"I am, but you started it. Glyptodont was a cousin of the arma-dillo."

The major pointed out that there would be no bones left.

"Nor of the master. Nor of his ship," I said. "Nor of Nodens nor Arthur nor the quick-witted Odysseus. But bones are not the only memorial."

In the afternoon we had to leave earlier than I intended in order to get off the mud. The ebb was still rolling down the river in a yellow flood, and Marrin's dinghy had not enough power to cross the tideway to the English Stones before we were carried down the Shoots. I was afraid that the first place we could put in to would be the port of Avonmouth but managed to bear away to starboard and anchor in the shelter of Gruggy Island which formed the right-hand bank of the gorge and was partly showing. There we had to stay for two more hours in full view of the Welsh coast until slack water. A passing coaster hailed us to know if we wanted help. I understood why Marrin only went out when low water was at night and kept his rowing boat in the mouth of the pill at New Passage.

When the force of the tide died away we crossed to the inlet in the Stones where we had been the night before and where I could change into full gear for the dive unobserved. At about seven the Shoots became as motionless as a pond and I went in carrying a small bag of stout canvas. The cave was not easy to find again, for I had been carried past it at speed and surfaced well to the north. When at last I saw it a good ten minutes of slack water had been wasted.

I swam into the mouth, keeping well clear of the bottom, though it was the usual Severn mixture of mud and sand and probably safe. Ahead of me my light showed a vertical face of rock about the height of a man which at first I thought was the end of the cave, but it wasn't. On the top of this little cliff was a flat ledge running back a few yards, with a slope to the right of it which ended in a nearly perpendicular funnel. It occurred to me even then that if this fissure carried on as it started it might end in a blowhole at the surface of the Stones.

The ledge had a floor of fine silt which did not appear to have been disturbed. I swept it away to reveal the bare rock beneath, but at the expense of being half blinded by the cloud I created. Below the cleft I touched something which I thought was an oddly shaped shell and pulled it out. It was encrusted with sea growths but so exactly ring-shaped that it had to be a man-made object. Time was forgotten. I was wild with excitement. I wriggled over the silt swashing a space all around me like a cock salmon looking for eggs to fertilize in the bed of a stream. I don't know what Marrin was after when he first entered the cave. It would not have been salmon but doubtless had something to do with life in the dark deep. He was very much in my mind, but without fear. I was conscious that I must be imitating all his movements. And then his hand had struck, as mine did, little flat pebbles which slid easily upon each other, scoured clean by the gentle wash of the silt.

I took two of them in my hand and sank down to the mouth of the cave where I was clear of the haze of silt and had a faint sheen of evening light from the surface. They were gold ingots, roughly the size and shape of a beech leaf and a quarter of an inch thick. Putting them in my bag along with the ring I returned to the back of the ledge where I had found them and cleared three neat blocks of ingots, which suggested that they had been tied together or packed in a wooden case. The outer surfaces of each block were heavily crusted with marine growth which had held it together.

With the thoughtless greed of gold fever I filled the bag, and of course found that the load and I could never reach the surface; so I put back a few ingots and then discarded the lead weights of my belt to the approximate equivalent of what was left in the bag. On swimming to the mouth of the cave I found that the tide had turned and was running more strongly than the day before. I was still below neutral buoyancy but able to come up then and there if I dropped either gold or lead. I chose lead rather than to lose forever several thousand pounds at the bottom of the Shoots. I came up all right, but to the roof of the cave, carried by a surging running into it. Back to the ledge I went, scraping along the roof and, lacking the experience of a professional diver, confused by the weight being in my hand, not around my waist.

Obviously I needed to be heavier in order to get clear of the cave mouth, and was about to add three or four ingots to my belt — since there was no hope of finding the discarded lead weights — when another of the intermittent surges caught me and washed me into the funnel. I could see through the water that far above me was light. I could also see that the cleft was not nearly wide enough for my body to go through. Panic-stricken scrapings with knees and elbows got me clear, and by the time the next surge arrived I was firmly anchored to the floor of the ledge, one hand in a deep crack and the other feeling for more gold to fill the bag and keep me down. I no longer cared how much of it was lost for good when I was safely out of the cave and could throw it away. Marrin's treasure had seemed likely to do a better job than he had done.

This time I was able to walk beyond the mouth of the cave and hung there pitching ingots into the interior until I was buoyant. Then the face of the gorge began to rush past and I surfaced at much the same point as the day before. The dinghy was too near the current of the flowing tide to be reached by swimming so I came ashore at the nearest outcrop of the Stones and walked and waded to Elsa and our little harbor.

She was less alarmed than the previous evening, assuming that what I had done once so easily I could do again. As for me, I had had enough and was determined not to dive in the Shoots again for all the gold of the Americas. I dropped the bag on the bottom of the dinghy and showed her the contents.

"So this is where the golden cauldron came from!" she exclaimed.

I replied that I was fairly sure it had not. All Marrin's deceptions were at last clear to me. He could not sell the ingots as they were without giving some explanation of the origin, and so he melted them down and made them into brooches, ashtrays and the rest which dealers would accept without question as the output of Broom Lodge.

"But then why the pretense of alchemy?" she said.

"Well, you once told me that he knew a lot about it and used to experiment at home. I think he used the mysterious origin of the gold to increase his hold on the inner circle, encouraging them to believe whatever they liked. He made the cauldron and it was for use at the ceremonies, not for sale. Even Sir Anthony Aslington was astonished by its strange beauty and the major considers the damned thing is holy."

"Any more glyptodonts?"

A wild but just possible guess occurred to me.

"No. But I may have found the pet's collar."

"I think it was for a woman's hair," she said, chipping away a crust. "The ends don't meet."

"They don't on a dog collar either."

"But they must have taken their wives on the ship."

"They took their wives and children to the highest ground and left them. And I'm not going back there to look for tiaras."

Elsa shuddered. My description must have been vivid.

"No! That horrible funnel!"

"There's just time to see if it comes to the surface," I said.

We left the dinghy and walked across the Stones to a point a little way back from the edge of the Shoots where a blowhole should appear if the cleft went right up through the rock. All the pools were motionless except one where the water and the floating weed pulsated up and down with an occasional spurt of foam.

It was now obvious to me why Marrin had never cleared the lot out at one go. Weight was the answer. He had no one to help him; he could never be dead sure of his time of arrival; and he would have found the same problem that I had — too heavy or too light and the fast tide ready to punish any miscalculation. So he decided to take no risks, leaving his treasure where it was and drawing on it in small quantities as required.

But I did have a helper. My determination never to dive again vanished. I had asked for trouble by arriving too late and staying too long. Provided I plunged in at the first sign of slack water and remained below for not more than ten minutes, there was little danger.

"If we had some sort of smooth cylinder that won't catch on the rock and lowered it down the blowhole at the end of a rope . . ."

"You are not to, Piers. You said you wouldn't."

"But this is easy. You at the top. Me at the bottom filling the cylinder. We can collect the lot in one dive, or two if the weight is too much."

"What are we to do with them?"

"I don't know. We'll work it out. There are so many duties."

The pools were filling now, and we had a longer and more devious walk back to our harbor, often with the rising tide rippling around our ankles. The dinghy was not there. I could see it a quarter of a mile away on its course for Gloucester.

It was my fault. I should have foreseen it. The dinghy was moored with the painter coiled round a large boulder at the far end of the inlet. Rendered half-witted by tiredness, excitement and the safe return to Elsa, I had never looked at the mooring when we walked off to find the pool. Meanwhile the rising tide had lifted the painter off the boulder.

Swimming was quicker than walking. I told Elsa to stay on a ridge of the Stones which would be the last to be covered, and struck out for the New Passage pill and Marrin's rowing boat. It was where the ebb had left it, high above the water on a slope of mud, fortunately steep. I was nearly up to my waist in it before my feet touched a strip of gravel at the bottom of the stream and the boat slid into the water.

"We'll never catch up with the dinghy," she said when I had rescued her.

"No. But wherever the tide takes her, it ought to take us."

She was no longer in sight, for it was after sunset. I rowed out to the point where I reckoned she would have been when we last saw her, shipped the oars and allowed the Severn to take over.

More embarrassment was to come. Evidently we had been

watched for some time from the Welsh coast and when the dinghy was seen floating away we were taken for two very foolish tourists stranded on the Stones and in danger of drowning. A boat was racing out and came alongside.

"That your dinghy what's gone upriver?" the boatman asked.

The last thing we wanted was for him to chug upriver ahead of us, overtake the dinghy and find out what I had been diving for. How right Marrin had been to confine his explorations to the hours of darkness!

"Don't you bother!" I said cheerfully. "We'll catch up with her in Slime Road."

I think he was impressed that I knew the name of the main channel on the right bank.

"If she don't go up Oldbury and come to grief on the rocks. I wouldn't bet on it. And what the goodness were 'ee doing on the Stones with all that underwater rubber on 'ee?"

"Fishing," I answered and was searching for the least improbable lie when Elsa piped up in a sweet little-girl voice:

"I wanted a swim and there wasn't anywhere else."

I took my cue and added apologetically:

"You know what women are."

"Serve you right! Where you from?"

"Chepstow. Came down on the tide."

"And that there boat?"

He couldn't possibly have seen me take it out from New Passage.

"Towing it, in case the girl wanted to go and bask on a sand-bank."

"What she want to do that for?"

"You see, I do love to sunbathe with nothing on," Elsa said. The boatman must have been a good Welsh Methodist, for he sheered off at once. If we were bound for hell anyway, it didn't make much difference when we drowned.

"Good night!" Elsa called. "And thank you for wanting to help us."

The fast flood had now swept us under Severn Bridge and into

Slime Road, so it had probably done the same for the dinghy. She'd be pretty safe there, bumping her way up from soft bank to soft bank. The tide was not yet high enough for shipping to be proceeding up channel. That was lucky. If the dinghy were picked up by some enterprising mariner and natural curiosity led him to see what was in the bag, we were not likely to hear any more of her — especially as my clothes were in the bottom indicating that the owner might have gone for a swim which was his last.

Twice we nosed into shore to examine possible dinghies; one turned out to be a stranded log and the other a drowned cow. We left it to the tide to do what it wished with us until we came to the tip of the Shepherdine Sands and had to make up our minds beteen the main channel and the Lydney channel. The boat, caught by a swirl, twisted round uncertainly three times until I backwatered and directed us, stern foremost, into the Lydney channel. Elsa, watching the wide and promising expanse of water on the other side of the sands, protested. I replied that the dinghy might have been caught by a similar whirlpool and that we should put our trust in Nodens and the Roman Manual for Pilots.

Neither let us down. The dinghy was aground, heeling over but still dry, just before the Guscar Rocks, her ghostly helmsman trying to make the vanished port of Woolaston.

There was nothing we could do but wait alongside her for the tide to rise, and ensure that she remained on an even keel until she was on the shale beach where Marrin and I had come ashore from the rocks. It was after midnight and not a sound but the suckings and splashings of the river. The dim line of the railway embankment cut us from the world.

Meanwhile we discussed what should be done with the twenty or so pounds of gold we had and the much larger quantity which remained in the cave.

"What do you think happened to them?" she asked.

"All we know is that the tribes of the marshes did not know what gold was and had no use for it. My guess is that the adventurers never returned to the cave or the ship, and that the pet of the voyage died there."

"Perhaps they were taken away and worshipped like the gods which Uncle Simeon was training the colonists to be."

"Or made the common mistake of the half-civilized in taking a dance of welcome for a war dance and opening fire with whatever weapons they had."

We moored the boats — safely this time — to a bush overhanging the bank, and slept a little in each other's arms on the short, sheep-nibbled grass of a Severn lawn.

"I could stay here forever," she said.

An express from South Wales hurtled past on the embankment, the roar and the lights reminding us that we were not on a private planet of green earth and salt water orbiting the Milky Way overhead, but in a demanding modernity from which relief could only be obtained by labor on the land and by pretenses, like those of Broom Lodge, that the world of machines did not or in the future would not exist.

First light was showing in the east and a cock broke the silence.

"Where do we go now?"

There at least I could answer her with certainty.

"Down on the ebb. We can't do anything else. We might try New Passage. Your uncle knew what he was doing, and if we pick up his mooring we can get off at half tide."

"You're going to try again?"

"We have two more days when the Stones will be well above water and it will be late dusk. After that we might have to wait a fortnight or a month to get it right."

True enough. But I was impatient to find more evidence, if there was any, rather than more ingots.

So New Passage it was. Dead tired and hungry we took an early bus to Bristol, where I bought an old army valise to carry the Aqualung and the rest. That was enough to persuade a hotel to accept two very shabby travelers whose only other possession was a bag containing enough wealth to buy the place.

When we were bathed, clean and breakfasted, some energy returned, and we wandered through the town searching antique shops in the hope of finding such a cylinder as I had in mind. Old leather buckets there were, but too wide. Umbrella stands of china, but they might break. A wooden roller of God knows what use, but the hollow center was not big enough. Eventually I bought the brass case of — I think — a six-inch naval shell which had been polished up and had an ashtray to match fitted to the top. I got the reluctant proprietor, proud of his ingenuity, to remove the ashtray and to bore three equidistant holes in the top to which the end of the rope could be attached. After that, fifty feet of rope was easy enough to find in a seaport and we returned with our purchases to the curious glances of a hotel porter who must have thought them odd for a pair of lovers.

Next day we went by train to Gloucester and bus to Bullo where we recovered my car and returned to Bristol. In the late afternoon we drove out to New Passage, took both boats off Marrin's mooring and anchored off the rippling dark water which covered the Stones to wait for the bottom of the tide in the late dusk. This time there was no risk of being watched from the Welsh coast, but while picnicking in the dinghy we were hailed three times to warn us of the invisible rocks.

They emerged from the sea like a herd of slow monsters, quickly uniting to become the flat and weedy desert of the English Stones. We made our usual inlet, then walked out to the blowhole where we lowered the shell case on the end of its rope. It was checked only once, easily clearing the obstruction, and we could feel it hit the bottom at a depth of forty feet.

As soon as there was no perceptible current in the Shoots I went in. No adventures or dangers of any sort this time. Our cylinder was resting on the slope which led up to the funnel. I loaded it with the remaining ingots and watched it disappear as Elsa pulled it up. That done, I searched the terrace for any other evidence of man, sweeping the silt gently and methodically away with my eyes and my torch so close that I could miss nothing. I found only two flint arrowheads of early Neolithic type: one close under the back wall, the other more or less in line and two yards out. That only proved that one or both parties had discovered the bow. I should have expected the immigrants to have it, but not necessarily the fishers and hunters along the Severn banks. Apart from the gold, there was no sign that the cave had ever sheltered man.

I came up before the turn of the tide. Elsa was staring at the pile of ingots she had emptied out of the shell case, their color still faintly showing gold in the starlight. I knew that my first haul had weighed about twenty pounds. This lot was double as much. So we had some sixty pounds in all.

"Broom Lodge must have some of it," she murmured, "since that was what Uncle Simeon wanted and so do I. But I'm damned if they get the lot! Have *you* got everything you have been risking your life for?"

"I've got everything I could want, my darling."

"I didn't mean a tall bit of nonsense with fair hair. Are you going to add a chapter to history and tell them seamen got here with gold soon after the melting of the ice?"

I said that I had not had time to think about it.

"Piers, who knows where our world is going? We too might have to sail off to the unknown with this as cargo."

"And sell it for half a deer and some sausages. Or shall we start up the first bank and credit ourselves with six hundred pounds a troy ounce?"

"Is that what it's worth?"

"Roughly four hundred thirty-two thousand pounds."

I had intended to take both boats up to Bullo with the tide. One reason was that the dinghy belonged to the commune and Dunwiddy would want to know what had happened to it: another reason was that the rowing boat could not remain much longer at New Passage without arousing curiosity. But when it came to the point I funked the voyage to Bullo. With a five-knot tide under me and as much again from the engine it could easily be done in four hours by any fisherman who knew the river, but I disliked the thought of navigating the channel in the dark and I was not at all sure whether I should reach the Horseshoe Bend before or after the bore. So I decided to put into Sharpness where Elsa would meet me with the car and the gold, and leave Bullo for another day.

That run to Sharpness with the boat in tow was I think, the most melancholy hour of my life. Yet so black a mood should have been impossible when I loved and was loved in return and had no financial worries. I foresaw the betrayal I mentioned at the outset of this report. A professional betrayal. I was bound in honor to put the ingots on show and publish the story of the find. But if I did so, my reputation as a serious scholar would be ruined. Despondency was of course affected by the high, black banks of both sides of the channel, cutting out all sights of the land and filling me with apprehension as if I were a shade alone in Charon's boat taking the ferry over to hell.

Science and folk memories agree that a great flood was fact, but the very reasonable assumption that some community progressing toward urban civilization might have been drowned is considered fantasy. Why? After all, London and New York within a few millennia will with absolute certainty be under either ice or the sea. Fantasy would be the accusation against me. An accusation, powered by jealousy perhaps, but unanswerable.

What was I to publish? What proof had I? I remember saying that bones were not the only memorial, but bones and artifacts, decently packed in the earth, at least give dates. I had found only two arrowheads, and had no evidence at all to prove that they were contemporary with the ingots though I believe they were. My theory, for what it's worth, is that the seamen took to the country fully armed. After the massacre two of the mortally wounded struggled back to the landing place and died side by side. The arrowheads in their bodies are all that remained. Laughable!

All laughable. I could hear the learned voices. In the patterns of the chop of the tide I could read the reviews: ". . . mere conjecture." "I am sorry that a man like Colet should have fallen for Atlantis." "All mixed up with a bunch of latter-day prophets he was." "Yes, I've been shown the ingots but I'm not impressed. Peruvian probably and from a wreck." "The glyptodont? Well, I'm told it's possible that the carapace could be preserved under the silt while the bones had of course disappeared. Pickled in salts, if I understood it. But what proof have we that Colet didn't find it among some curios in a shop?" "I hear he had the impudence to go to the British Museum with a gold bowl which was made yesterday."

I decided that I could not publish, that I must leave my proofs — which are not proofs — to some later time when other discoveries may incline archaeologists to accept my story.

I swear that my motives were not hypocritical. I am not in the least afraid of giving the details of how I was led to the Shoots; it would be easy to leave out the irrelevancies of the den and of the deaths of Marrin and Evans. And I did not decide to keep my mouth shut because my wife would be stinking rich if I did. I kept it shut because I had nothing to add to history, and belief in my adventurers from the ocean would be damaged rather than confirmed.

Elsa was at Sharpness and ran down the water steps to greet my arrival.

"You met a bit of spray," she said as she kissed me.

Running with the tide there was no spray. It seems that I can become overwrought when forced to choose, so much alone, between two alternatives equally detestable.

We had to wait till dawn for the dinghy to enter the canal behind a little freighter with a sweet-smelling cargo of timber. Then we set off for London, placed our wealth in a metal deedbox which had belonged to my grandfather and deposited it to join the cauldron in the bank, devoid of any idea what to do with either.

After a day's rest in the flat with my delicious girl, so level-headed in all but love, we drove down to Sharpness again to take the boats up to the Bullo mooring on the morning tide. While we were sitting in the sun on that lawn, exclaiming like a pair of children at the lovely product of nothing but silt and sheep, she asked:

"Do you think we could go and see what's happened at Broom Lodge?"

"You, but not me. They mustn't see any connection between you and me and Wigpool."

"Suppose the major has been chucked out?"

"If he has been, take care that you are never alone and get out quick!"

I didn't like it, but I knew that the commune was still a part of her life. When we first fell in love she had protested at being considered "maternal." But in fact her feeling toward Broom Lodge was inevitably maternal. She could not be expected to keep away.

"It will be all right. I'm still Saint Elsa," she said

"But Saint Elsa has the cauldron."

"That's why I ought to show myself. And I have a good excuse. I need my clothes and things."

I stopped close to the colony, and she walked the rest of the way as if she had just come down from Gloucester by bus. Then I concealed the car under the oaks — I was getting quite good at that — and took up my old post in the foxgloves where I could watch the back of the house.

The major had not been chucked out. She led him around the west wing where I could see him. To my amazement he had adopted the tonsure of the druidicals. Was he following the practice of the Celtic church and had Arthur gone pagan? No doubt he had a good reason and no doubt I should not be able to understand it.

She took my advice and did not stay long. When she returned with a suitcase in each hand she told me that she had not seen any of the six but had been received with touching affection by all the ordinary members of the commune whom she had met. Denzil had warned her that affairs were critical but that he would not give up. "Give up what?" she asked, and had only got the typical reply that he was not worthy. She tried to tell him that we knew the origin of her uncle's gold and had the lot. He was not interested. She had the impression that he was busy with some spiritual awakening of the colonists and that finance was of no importance. Nothing was yet safe, he told her, and the pagans must be delivered from temptation, so she had better clear off. He would come to the den in the afternoon. Choice of the den seemed to indicate that the druidicals were wandering through the bracken as irresponsibly as frightened pigs and might interrupt us at the old rendezvous of the sapling stump.

After a quick lunch we went up to the den. It was much as I had left it. Again I was threatened by the melancholy of disappointment and had to shake it off. I had spent so long there, hot on the track of the mysterious cauldron. It had indeed been a Grail for me, to be revealed through danger, discomfort and the reverence of the seeker. Perhaps that is the essential mystery of any Grail. It exists, but when you know it exists, it exists no longer.

The major turned up, climbing the slope in the heat of the afternoon with the determination of the wandering friar he called himself. In the depths of his eyes, somewhat fishlike in his club, shining in the forest, I could see that he was carrying the shield of Arthur into battle.

"I need a miracle, old boy," he said.

I answered that I had run through several miracles in the last few days and hadn't one left.

"Do they still believe I pinched the ornaments?" Elsa asked.

"Doesn't matter. Executor chap called Dunwiddy has been after me. I told him how we'd found the bag digging out a new rubbish pit and were short of cash. Right, he says, we'll sell 'em, major. He knew the name of the firm which bought from Simeon, so we took the bag up to town. Glad to see us, they were. Weighed. Assayed. Paid by check to late Mr. Marrin's executors. No questions asked. Broom Lodge products well known. Clever devil, Simeon was."

It was my failure to see how the commune made a profit which first set me off. Elsa was not so astonished. She knew her uncle did sell his wares but no more. Whenever Broom Lodge needed money, it had been transferred from Marrin's personal account which she never saw.

"No reason why you should. Laundry. Catering. Sales of meat and vegetables. Shoulder to cry on. But uncle's private account not your business and not the commune's."

"You mean that all his work in gold had a market?" Elsa asked.

I didn't see why she should look at me with such sudden intensity, but the major was prompt to understand.

"Give us half. Installments as and when. Is it a deal?"

"Done! But there isn't a goldsmith among the lot."

"Will be, if I have my way. What do you think I've gone bald for, Piers?"

"God knows."

"He does. You're right. Solidarity, that's why. I'm showing sympathy with the opposition. Beats them! They're as curious as cats. Look here! All those decent chaps at Broom Lodge haven't any religion. A pity, but there it is! I'd call 'em well-meaning agnostics. All that reincarnation stuff just makes them feel good. The only truly pious are the druidicals and myself. Their religion is sincere but their rites are degrading. How do you think the missionaries converted the Saxons? Started with a pagan priest of course. Converted him, and the other fellows followed."

"Elsa!" I appealed. "Will you please tell me what the hell Denzil is talking about?"

"But it's simple, darling. You haven't a business mind. We've solved the problem of getting rid of the gold without certificates and all sorts of papers we can't get. Half for Broom Lodge. Half for us."

"But what has it got to do with goldsmiths?"

"I'll take 'em off wrought iron and give 'em six months training," Denzil explained. "Elsa supplies the gold. When we sell the gewgaws, half the proceeds to Broom Lodge. Half to her. Have to work it out."

"Suppose what they make isn't salable?"

"Who cares? It's bought for the gold. For all I know, the buyers throw the rest away."

Now that was close to what Marrin had actually told me.

"But it all depends on your mission to the pagans."

"That's where solidarity comes in."

"You'll fetch up on the altar at Wigpool."

"Not if I can work a miracle."

"I don't wonder a theological college threw you out. In the Middle Ages you'd have been flayed alive for blasphemy."

"It's not blasphemy at all," he answered indignantly. "To convert the heathen a miracle is permissible. At least two saints crossed the Irish Sea on stones that floated."

"And if you can pull it off, are you going to be abbot of Broom Lodge?"

"Not me. Raeburn has the makings of an abbot. He's deeply religious and the sort of chap I'd go into the jungle with."

"And not come out."

"I think that if I returned the cauldron . . ." Elsa began.

"Good girl!"

"And if I could return it in such a way that you had your miracle . . ."

"Better and better!"

"Pity it won't float," I said. "But we might send it over the river in a toy boat."

He was really angry with me now.

"Not a game! It's not a game at all. There must be true reverence."

"For a fraud?"

"For what it creates. Simeon knew that."

"Don't fuss, Piers!" Elsa ordered me. "You aren't the bloody Inquisition. Dear Denzil, are you sure you can make them start training to be goldsmiths?"

"No. But you can."

"How long must I stay?"

"A week should do it. What do they call that thing which turns one stuff into another? A catalyst, that's it. Well, you're the catalyst."

I was frankly shocked, but realized that with Saint Elsa's help our fifth-century Paladin might be able to pull off his revolution. The druidicals were in disarray. Their high priest had died; his succesor had been drowned; the gods were angry. While the rest of the commune was indifferent to any nonsense they might get up to, the major at least showed a sign of sympathy by his shaven head.

Denzil no longer believed that the cauldron was the Grail, but he did in some sense believe that its shape and its strange gold partook of the ancient myth. That was what the druidicals, encouraged by Marrin, had believed. So the violently heretical Christian and the pious pagan could agree on its sanctity so long as neither insisted on exact definitions.

Take my old friend Nodens as a half-absurd example. Whether I call him Nodens or an angel makes no difference to anybody. The essential is that I do not wholly deny a Something Else able to influence me. On that Something Else a fifth-century missionary could build, whereas he would have been helpless before a pure materialist — who didn't exist anyway.

This attempt to comprehend the incomprehensible major by way of Nodens brought the god to mind. Spirit of land and river, healer, restorer of lost property and in his relations with me undoubtedly a god of mischief, he should find a miracle within his powers. Summoned by my thought of him, he remarked — as always through my imagination — that druids were not likely to be familiar with diving and it might be possible to stage a marvel more convincing than a toy boat — or a stone one if it came to that.

The major hurried back to his secular duties, which he was taking very seriously. He only knew a little about agriculture and nothing whatever about the crafts, but his military life had taught him that discipline can be imperceptible. He made no attempt to replace that benevolent dictator, Marrin. He merely organized committees and stood back.

"You shouldn't have been so rough with him," Elsa said. "You know he's crackers."

"He's not crackers. You just have to decide which century his memory is in while the rest of him is here and now. One half sees pets. The other half commits burglary."

"Anyway, he saw how we could get rid of our gold before you did."

"If he can get his amateur alchemists to work. And that depends on the miracle."

"But I've made our fortune, Piers! And you aren't excited, just dreaming."

"I am wondering what can give me the exact time when half the blasted Severn is going uphill to Gloucester and the other half going downhill to the Shoots and it's high water at the Box Rock. Nodens and I will then produce a miracle while you, sweet Saint Catalyst, do your vestal-virgin stuff on the bank. So back to London and get the Grail out of pawn!"

I have an old friend whose hobby is vintage cars. By day he is an archaeologist, at night a motor mechanic. It seems to be a point of honor that one must rebuild every part as it originally was. To put in a new engine, a new transmission or anything new is as disgraceful as to salt a dig with bones which don't belong to it. Consequently his workshop is a museum of bits and pieces.

I called on him with Elsa. It was the first time she had appeared to a normal friend in my normal life. She was looking as innocently alluring as an advertisement in a Sunday supplement and he couldn't take his eyes off her.

"I want a thin steel rod," I told him, "painted black and about ten feet long, firmly fixed to a plate at one end with a quick-release clamp at the other."

"What has the clamp got to take?"

"The bottom rim of this, and it had better be padded."

I took the cauldron out of its hat box and showed it to him.

"What an exquisite thing!" he exclaimed. "Persian and about sixth century B.C. I would say."

I was glad of that. It showed that a better authority than I could be taken in. I had been feeling a little humiliated since the verdict of the British Museum.

"It's only a modern replica. Lead gold-plated."

"But what for?"

I was momentarily stuck for a lie, but Elsa was not.

"My cousin's birthday," she said. "They're filthy rich. Jet set and all that. So I had to have something original."

He looked at me ironically as if wondering how a serious economist could have got mixed up with a crazy bunch of conspicuous consumers.

"I've got a bit of just the right rod. Strong as a Toledo blade. Come and have a look at it, Piers!"

He led me through a pool of oil round the back of a vast landaulet.

"So you've been out baby-snatching! What a stunner! She looks like the Dea Roma on holiday."

"I'm the baby more often than not."

"Where did you find it?"

"Salmon fishing."

"Not your style unless you were trying to find how much Julius Caesar paid for a pound. When does she want this device of hers?"

"As soon as possible."

"She would! Well, it's all straightforward except for the quick-release clamp. I'll have to look around for that."

"And you must let me make a subscription to your old-age pensioners."

"It won't be expensive. But this one would be grateful, wouldn't you?" He slapped the glossy flank of the landaulet. I wonder he didn't blow up its nose.

When we were home again — what enchantment to be able to write "home" instead of "my flat"! — Elsa's curiosity was of course unbounded, but I refused to tell her what I was planning.

"Because I need your inspiration when you see it for the first time. That's decisive — far more important than anything else. Is it a miracle or is it not? If there's any doubt, we've had it and you might be in trouble."

She accepted this nobly, and I was allowed to spend a few evenings in the home for senile motors making a light raft with a float attached to each side to keep it level. When the ten-foot rod was ready, with its plate at one end and its clamp at the other, I tied the lot on top of my car, recovered the cauldron from the bank and told Elsa it was time to go down to Gloucester.

"Oh, not Gloucester again!" she exclaimed.

"Well, the Thames is too crowded. But up the Severn somewhere we ought to find a bit of peace in the dusk."

"Thank God it's not that horrible tideway!"

"Not yet. And if all goes well and you approve, we'll stay the night and have a conference with the major next day."

The map suggested that the Haw Bridge, some six miles above Gloucester, might do for the rehearsal of my experiment. When we got there, the evening river was not as peaceful as I expected, so we walked along the bank carrying with us the raft, the rod, the hatbox and all my equipment for diving until we found a spot a little upstream from the bridge where no pleasure cruisers were moored and there was a good screen of bushes between the towpath and the fields. I asked Elsa to cross the bridge, follow the far bank until she was opposite to me and then to watch the gently flowing current and report what she saw.

Meanwhile I changed and assembled the miracle — a mere matter of screwing to the center of my raft the plate at the bottom of the rod and clamping the cauldron to the top. Then I pushed the raft out to deep water and reduced the pressure in the floats until the base of the cauldron was just awash.

It was now dusk, permitting no clear view at a distance but quite enough light to see any floating object. Keeping on the same level as the raft I pushed it in front of me underwater until it grounded. That did not matter. It would never ground at all off the Box Rock.

I stood up and removed the mask, waiting for the vital comment. Elsa was clapping.

"I could swear it floated across the river on its own. I could just see the rod once or twice but I'm sure I wouldn't have if I hadn't known it was there. And on the tideway ripples and a bit of spray will hide the bottom. It left a little wash behind even on the calm river. Denzil will believe it's a real miracle. Dare we let him?"

I said I'd love to. His reactions would be so fascinating. But he had to be in the secret in order to organize the reception party.

We returned to our hotel where Elsa called up the major to make an appointment for the next day. He said he would meet us in the afternoon at the sapling stump — which indicated that by now the druidicals had returned to the routine of the commune instead of wandering disconsolately through the woods.

In the morning I visited the port offices to find out when it would be high water at Box Rock — a question apparently that

[*178*

only the river could answer. I was told that at Sharpness and Lydney there could be no doubt, but within the Horseshoe Bend it might depend on the wind. Since the tides were now neap there would be little or no bore. At the Box Rock and Bullo the top of the tide — give or take ten minutes — should be about 8:50 P.M. the day after tomorrow and the slack water wouldn't last long. It would not yet be high tide at Gloucester, but the ebb would certainly have started below the Noose.

We found the major at the sapling stump looking military but not to the extent of visionary stirrups. I explained to him how the cauldron would cross the river and asked if he could guarantee that his six pagans would be on the bank just upstream from the Box Rock on Thursday at half past eight; they might have to chant or meditate for half an hour or more until the dusk was of the right texture.

I could see that his conscience bothered him. A miracle he had asked for, but not such a bare-faced miracle. He sighed but, yes, he was sure the party could be arranged at the right time provided Elsa returned with him now to Broom Lodge and mixed normally with the colonists.

"Carry on as if no inner circle existed, just like your uncle."

"Are they likely to bow to me as they pass?" Elsa asked.

"I'll settle that with Raeburn."

"Good God!" I exclaimed. "Is he installed already?"

"He is high priest. The rest will follow."

"Has Elsa got to preach to them?"

"Not her job, old boy! That's where I come in. All Elsa has to do is to visit the blacksmith's shop and tell them they must learn to work in gold, that gold came before tin and is far more sacred. She will show them a sign."

"What about the training?"

"Club porter. Nothing he doesn't know. I'll ask him to find me a young goldsmith who'd like the job. And must be an earnest Christian."

"We have to find a way of delivering the raw material."

"Darling, the priestess looks after that. I think the cauldron should not be empty. We'll put a few ingots in it and I shall scatter them in the meadow like Flora with a cornu-what's-it."

"But we haven't any ingots with us."

"Yes we have. I always carry three in my bag for luck."

I told the major to see that their torches were alight, and flaming red. As the marvel approached, Elsa would walk into the water, being very careful not to step over the edge into the Box Hole, undo the clamp — she had already practiced that — and display the cauldron.

"Do I beckon to it, or what?"

"Just hold out your hands as if you knew it were coming. Do whatever you feel like. You were so magnificent at Wigpool. Nothing that I suggest could be as good."

"Never did like night operations," the major grumbled. "Always go wrong."

But it was not really the operation which was disturbing him.

"Tell me, Piers! In your heart do you believe I am justified in this grave step?"

"I do. The end justifies the means. What would Arthur have been without Merlin? And how would the Household Cavalry impress the public if they rode in battle dress instead of the masquerade of plumes and breastplates?"

That cheered him up a bit, and so we parted. The next I should see of Elsa — well, I should never see her at all until it was safe to show my head above water. I comforted myself with the thought that if the miracle misfired we could always swim to whatever safety the Severn offered.

On Thursday evening I drove to Arlingham and down the lane to the river. When the few tourists had gone and my car was the only one left, I walked along the embankment till I was above the tail of the sands and nearly opposite the Box Rock. The tide was rising fast over a good stretch of muddy beach and, as usual, I was quite alone. Two journeys brought out from the car my underwater gear, the cauldron and its raft.

After sunset I had a lot of work to do on the floats. On the upper river I had taken the cauldron across empty, not remembering that in the tideway it would soon fill with water. Since I could not tell how much would splash into it, I filled it full before the start and added Elsa's ingots.

The distance across the river to the Box Rock was rather more than half a mile of which the last three hundred yards were deep water and the rest shoals. I had to walk or swim over these banks until I could reach the channel. That was a difficulty I had not foreseen. The force of the tide was too great for it to be done, and there was not enough water to float the raft at its proper depth. The only hope was to go in much farther downriver where the channel swung over to the left bank and allow the tide to carry me up.

This move toward Hock Cliff wasted more time but was all to the good, for the summer evening was still too light for my purpose. I came to rest on the sands opposite the Box Rock and looked across the river to the meadow alongside it. I could distinguish no more than moving figures, among them one in white which had to be Elsa. So it was safe to stay where I was, showing only head and shoulders, until slack water at the top of the tide, when I could be sure of keeping a straight course to the rock or very near it. Dead calm was essential for I dared not show my head.

Once I had set off and was underwater I was desperately convinced that this blind navigation could not possibly work, but more or less it did. I knew that my former, deadly exploration of the Box Hole would be useful and kept sounding for depth, allowing cauldron and raft to float on by themselves. I hit the rock too far upstream, turned along it and then had difficulty keeping the raft close enough in, so that I knew I must be right over the Box Hole and that the ebb had begun. I felt the raft tip a little. That ought to be Elsa removing the cauldron and deliberately shaking the rod to let me know. At once I threw my weight — nearly neutral but just enough — on to the raft in order to sink the top of the rod below water. Looking up, all I could see was a rippling surface tinged with red from the torches.

Curiosity was uncontrollable. I could not bear to be blind any longer. I felt my way inshore to a point where the bank was lower and I could see around the back of the rock to the meadow. Folly! But I hoped that in the fast-failing light I would be mistaken for a tree trunk if anyone glanced my way.

I need not have worried. The scene was beyond my fantasies, and how many faiths and legends were embodied in it was beyond conjecture. The torches flamed red in a semicircle, and in front of them Elsa, spreading the white wings of her sleeves, was holding out the cauldron to Raeburn, who was on his knees. The major too was on his knees. I cannot guess in what time his mind was. His mission, in his dreams, was to the pagans. It was now so in reality. I suppose that symbols are what you make of them. For the moment the Guardian of the Grail was present at its return.

Gravely Raeburn distributed the ingots. More effective and more hopeful that was than the Flora act which Elsa had contemplated. There was some conversation. Elsa appeared to dismiss the party and to bless them. She stood on the rock, still and statuesque, until they had crossed the railway embankment and were out of sight. I appeared from the mud. If there had been anyone to see us it would have been thought that she had summoned her tame sea monster.

She was overcome with the splendor of her own impersonation, nervous as an actress in the wings after triumph in a profoundly emotional scene. I wished I had champagne and half a florist's shop to go with my congratulations.

"Nearly disaster! So nearly!" she cried. "The rod rose too far out of the water. I covered it by flapping my sleeves. Then you must have dragged it down again. Thank God we have got away with it and they've gone!"

"But how did they think you would get home?"

"Saints don't take cars, darling. Think of me sitting in the back and chatting all the way to Broom Lodge! What shall we do?"

The ebb was running dangerously under the rising moon. It was impossible to swim across, but Bullo with Marrin's two boats on their moorings was less than half a mile away.

"We'll swipe the rowing boat. I can make it look as if the painter had chafed and broken."

The tide swept us from the pill, around the sands and softly under Hock Cliff, where I chose the steep beach of shale, its top just showing, rather than the shelf of rock which I knew too well. I set the boat adrift and we began to walk along the embankment toward the track where I had left my car, over grass, here long and studded with wildflowers, while the power of the fast ebb slid by our feet without sound or ripple. Her robe was wet and heavy at the hem. She took it off, flung it over her shoulder and after a few strides let it drop to the ground.

I remember how in that moment desire of her was most strangely mixed with awe, for she looked a spirit risen from the depths of the Severn still impatient for more worship.